SUN, S

AND SH

20 GREAT

SHORT

SUN, STONE, AND SHADOWS

20 GREAT MEXICAN SHORT STORIES

Edited by
Jorge F. Hernández

Contents

Introduction

JORGE F. HERNÁNDEZ

Perhaps literature is the best lens through which to observe Mexico's soul. And of all genres, perhaps the short story is the vehicle best suited for rendering snapshot scenes, actual places, words that have been shared by generations or forgotten by time, and above all, flesh-and-blood portraits of Mexicans that are perfectly credible—even when they're no more than inventions of ink on paper—whose biographies are eternal, precisely because they've been read.

I am talking about stories set among *Sun, Stone, and Shadows*; stories composed of plots and characters, scenarios and denouements, as well as authors who are reflected and refracted in the paragraphs they've written. All the other genres that literature branches into, such as the novel, essay, poetry, or even theater, could attempt to portray the soul of Mexico. But this anthology has taken it upon itself to require the reader's concentration on works of short fiction, stories that can be read in a single sitting, either during the daily bus or subway commute, or as long as it takes to wait for anything that doesn't succeed in leaving us behind schedule.

The twenty stories united in this anthology are the works of great Mexican writers born from 1887 to 1939. They are a sample—one that is, perhaps, neither exhaustive nor unique—of the best Mexican literature published during the first half of the twentieth century. Their roll call of authors is like a Pleiades of the best writers of contemporary Hispanic-American literature, some of them still living and continuously in print. Like all anthologies, ours was compelled to trim back the vast literary richness at hand: not a few authors were excluded who, though not born in Mexico, chose to not only live, write, and even die there, but also to filter Mexican enchantment and disenchantment into their works. This is the reason we do not present here any of the extraordinary tales by Gabriel García Márquez, Álvaro Mutis, José de la Colina, Max Aub, Julieta Campos, Alejandro Rossi, Augusto Monterroso, and other masters of the Mexican short story who, while belonging to the same era, were born in and share their nationality with other territories. Also excluded were authors born after 1939, in order to set that particular year as a mid-century date, although others could have served our purpose just as well. In order to counterbalance these subjective criteria, the twenty authors included in these pages compose a literary geography of sorts: their places of birth span nearly all of contemporary Mexico's regions, climates, and cultural and atmospheric zones.

Some readers might argue, timeline in hand, that the twentieth century was born with the champagne bubbles of the first minute of the year 1901. Others would insist that in the rest of the Western world as in Mexico, the twentieth century dawned with the bullets and cries of the first social revolution of the modern era: that compendium of clashes and rebellions we've come to know as the Mexican Revolution. This anthology signals our belief that a collection of stories by Mexican writers from the first half of the twentieth century must consider authors born during the final decades of the nineteenth century, when the long dictatorship of Porfirio Díaz was still paving circumstances, pending a generational change that proved to be just as inevitable as it was incontrollable, once the first shots of the revolution were fired. For over thirty years, General Porfirio Díaz wielded his authoritarian dictatorship by committing electoral fraud, appointing judges according to whim, censoring the press or any other critique of his power—while at the same time underscoring his fervent goal to modernize Mexico by installing a generalized peace, even at the cost of unanswerable repression, hoping to elevate the country to the same economic level as the industrialized world. It was as if the so-called "Porfirian Utopia" had determined that Mexico's gaze be turned solely towards the future and abroad. Yet this *esprit de temps*—despite its hypnotizing credo of progress and modernization—disdained the hunger of millions of dispossessed people, as well as the aspirations of young Mexicans who knew themselves to be sufficiently mature to govern their own destinies.

As the first decade of the twentieth century came to a close, Francisco I. Madero—a young liberal from northern Mexico with democratic ideals—challenged the dictatorship of Porfirio Díaz not only by beating him at the polls but also by making a subsequent call to arms. Madero managed to topple Díaz's government and become one of the youngest presidents in our history. Madero eventually was assassinated before completing his presidential term at the bloody hands of military officials and aristocrats who longed for the Porfirian Utopia's return. However, a fundamental change in national optics was already palpable in Mexico: the country would no longer necessarily point its gaze towards the future of progress, but towards the glories of its past. National projects would concentrate less and less on foreign ideas and models, and more and more on proposals that emanated from within. After Madero died, a wide array of forces focused their commitment on avenging his democratic sacrifice and fighting those who intended to drive the country backwards: Venustiano Carranza, under the banner of the need for a new constitution; Pancho Villa, an overwhelmingly popular bandit turned libertarian; and Emiliano Zapata, a peasant whose gaze went beyond any metaphorical expression of the unrest of the most impoverished masses. All three would contribute to overthrowing the government of usurpers that had killed Madero, and all three would take an active role in multiple disputes and bloodbaths that occurred, even among the *revolucionados* themselves, until the Revolution—now with a capital *R*—was able to lay down its arms and establish itself as a solid, irrefutable form of government.

Many revolutionary leaders and their followers wouldn't live to see the Revolution evolve into institutions: either by building new socio-economic structures or by founding a single political party that, while sidestepping the dictatorship of a single man, opened up the possibility that one party would govern Mexico for over seventy years—forty years longer than Porfirio Díaz himself, no less. Like a hall of mirrors, for seven decades of the twentieth century, the government of Mexico thwarted democracy through electoral fraud as well as any dictatorship, while at the same time fomenting the development of Mexico as a modern nation, stabilizing nearly all social unrest and spearheading many popular endeavors. The Revolution also bestowed its renewed creative spirit on its writers and other artists. Painters like Diego Rivera, José Clemente Orozco, and David Alfaro Siqueiros used their brushes to cover the walls of public buildings, with the general idea of recognizing the wealth of Mexico's past and all that had been disdained by the dictatorship.

The first half of the twentieth century in Mexico—decades that define the stories included in this anthology, as well as the lives of their authors—could be portrayed as an era of economic and industrial growth, urban expansion, and modernization. It was an era that also opened up the country's borders, making it a safe haven for victims of fascism and the world wars, especially Spanish Civil War refugees. The coin had been tossed into the air, and both heads and tails proved advantageous: Mexican nationalism and a deep pride in the roots of the past were used to advance many facets of national progress, while our universities, publishing houses, newspapers, and art galleries greatly benefited from the arrival of poets, novelists, teachers, and common laborers in exile from Spain and Europe as a whole.

The decades leading up to the crucial year of 1968 confirm this view of a two-sided reality that could very well also explain the literature included in this book. While the revolutionary governments of Mexico continued nurturing the consolidation of a modern nation, many local politicians continued sowing the seeds of corruption and abuse. The writers in this anthology were witnesses, or rather, heirs to this bipolar legacy. They inherited the rich culture of deep, historic roots and also saw themselves and their works cross universal artistic borders. Alfonso Reyes and Martín Luis Guzmán, who witnessed and suffered firsthand the bloody, revolutionary days, later saw their works translated and appreciated by other nations. Writers from the next generation, like Octavio Paz or Juan Rulfo, were the sons of direct survivors of the Revolution. As authors, they gained worldwide recognition during the late 1960s. The next generational segment spans from Carlos Fuentes to José Emilio Pacheco, both of whom continue to dazzle readers from around the world today, having written and lived through Mexico's opening up towards the modern trends of the Western world, traversing the rough patches of the Cold War, and culminating with the tragic events of 1968—when the Mexican government crushed a spirited student movement that demanded democracy during the massacre at the plaza of Tlatelolco. Two sides of the same coin: just ten days after the military crackdown, in the midst of a colorful gala, Mexico hosted the Olympic games.

The present anthology was guided by a desire to portray —insofar as possible—the diversity of Mexico. Here are tales of urban themes as well as stories that reflect the voices and ways of the fields and harvests. These pages offer circumstances that no longer exist, or no longer represent the unmistakable pigmentation of a Mexico that still remains beneath the skin of its masses. Here, the rage or shootings of past eras join together with the ecumenical illusions or secular imagination of the modern storyteller.

While there can never be too many, or even enough, anthologies of Mexican stories, several very good ones already exist in Spanish and in other languages. Although the task of determining a table of contents for this anthology may have seemed impossible beyond the obvious criteria—ordering the stories by the authors' dates of birth, or by their respective dates of publication—a thematic division into five areas of four stories each was made, keeping in mind each author's complete works, or the specific tone of the story chosen for these pages. The volume begins with four stories that flourish within "The Fantastic Unreal," followed by narrations that paint "Scenes from Mexican Reality." Next come those short stories that are, perhaps, most faithful to "The Tangible Past," and four more that tackle "The Unexpected in Everyday, Urban Life." The anthology concludes with another quartet that partakes of the purest "Intimate Imagination." Readers may choose to reshuffle the stories provided here, digesting them at will. Yet I'm certain the tides of chance have brought us a compilation that respects generational synchronizations, affinities, and traits, reaffirming the multicultural richness of Mexican literature.

This collection renders tales of the dispossessed and forgotten, together with the prepotent and potentate. And also the lives of those who lay claim to an honorable middle ground: the broad Mexican middle class that was consolidated during the first half of the twentieth century—the anonymous trajectory of characters who could have been so many others but who suddenly, somehow, endure through the permanent ink of the unforgettable story. This is about creating a kaleidoscope of short stories easy enough for any reader from any social background to read. This collection presents a dignified enclave of the best writers and tales of Mexico, whose translation into other languages will develop into a faithful photograph (whether in black and white, or color) of Mexico's varied faces, its flavors and colors, the deceased murmurs or larger-than-life screams that define us. It may be useful for the reader to keep in mind that Mexico is a land of enduring contrasts. The indelible religious fervor that all Mexicans display (particularly in their devotion to the Virgin of Guadalupe) remains intact through passing centuries, but it is engulfed by an ongoing binge of highly pagan forms of expression. Mexicans can let their hair down and pray at the same time. Our country boasts the luxury and ostentation of the wealthiest millionaires on the same streets where the impoverished and hungry stretch out the palms of their hands in despair. We Mexicans can celebrate life in every conversation, and honor all things living through different artistic expressions, while remaining solemnly faithful in our steadfast consideration of Death. Unlike Halloween, where you put on a disguise and take a chance on requesting a treat, here in Mexico we not only pay visits to our dead with flowers and fruit, food and drink (to be served and savored on their tombstones), we are also capable of giving our family and friends sugar skulls with their names written in candy on top, to celebrate the fact that they continue to live by our sides, while reminding them—and reminding ourselves—that some-day, we will walk the earth no more.

Perhaps for the same reason, the best tales of Mexican literature are not rosy, and our stories aren't prone to having happy endings. Like all good literature, Mexican letters—particularly Mexican short stories—are portraits of a reality that doesn't deny pain, despair, disgrace, deceit, bloodshed or desolation, although by that I don't mean to insinuate that Mexican reality is inevitably violent, or merely a chronology of pre-ordained disgraces. On the contrary, it signifies that our writers—perhaps more so than our other artists—weigh the contrasts of the unrest that lurks behind our constant joys, the tinge of melancholy that distills our smiles, the ongoing desire that we're capable of rendering to a lover who has forgotten that we exist.

Mexico is a country filled with stories, whether true stories or pure fiction. We greet our fellow man by asking him to tell us a tale. But, on the other hand, we can also snub our neighbor with the admonition that he's just telling tales. More than one politician or housewife upholds the Mexican saying that it's more important to tell tales than to take tolls, and in the vast majority of our homes, a story continues to be announced when in reality, a joke is about to be told. Quite a few of the writers gathered in this anthology have stated that their stories, or at least their first drafts, were written in a single sitting, either typed or by hand. Scribbled in green ink on yellowing sheets or set down by the nervous clacking that typewriters used to make, these are stories meant to be read as if you were leisurely drawing out an after-dinner conversation, or narrating mile after mile of a voyage while lost in a purple dusk, or

JORGE F. HERNÁNDEZ

remembering pieces of your life under the spell of the hypnotic insomnia with which subway cars move in Mexico City.

These twenty stories won't deprive anyone of reading comfort due to excessive length, or the viscosity of their respective plots and characters. They are easily understandable despite all the time that has passed since their initial publication. Their paragraphs, even translated, will tattoo themselves onto any reader's sensibility. They require no rigid timelines offering historical contexts, nor should they be entirely ascribed to the complete works, or other books, that these authors have published. For example: this anthology includes a single, magnificent story, one of the few fictional accounts ever written by Octavio Paz, one of the greatest Mexican poets of all time, universally known for his essays and poems. Likewise, extraordinary stories have been selected that were penned by authors like Carlos Fuentes and Salvador Elizondo, whose literary transcendence and editorial importance have been determined by their novels or novellas, all of which surpass the customary confines of the short story. There are also, albeit against the grain, stories that best exemplify the work of those who owed their very existence to the short stories they were dedicated to writing; authors like Edmundo Valadés or Juan José Arreola, who never found it necessary to venture out onto the unlimited plains of the novel, or the living stage of the theater, or to thread lines into delicate verses, or to try and reveal their own imaginations through the essay. Rather, they expressed themselves through the short story and, along the way, they expressed different facets of Mexico, like someone on a night train in Europe attempting to describe to a travel companion where he comes from and where his affections lie, what food is the kind he misses because it's nowhere to be had, and which words, just by being uttered, can make him cry for sheer joy.

Sun, Stone, and Shadows: 20 Great Mexican Short Stories has gone to press thanks to His Excellency Arturo Sarukhan, Ambassador of Mexico to the United States, whose leadership advanced this ground-breaking project. I want to express my appreciation also to Juan García de Oteyza and Hernán Bravo Varela, at the Mexican Cultural Institute in Washington, D.C., for their original ideas, and to Consuelo Sáizar, Joaquín Díez-Canedo, Martí Soler and Juan Carlos Rodríguez, at the Fondo de Cultura Económica, for their publishing savvy. The views and encouragement of Dana Gioia, Chairman of the National Endowment for the Arts in the United States, are greatly appreciated. Together with our partners, we are bringing the best of Mexican literature to both our nations.

This collection of stories would have been impossible without the collaboration of other editors, translators, and the authors themselves. This debt of gratitude is hereby extended to the poet Francisco Hernández, who helped assemble a long, initial list of short stories and writers that was later subjected to several rounds of selection and the inevitable criterion of exclusion. This arduous adventure was launched and ably completed by Clarissa Minchew and Pablo Duarte through hard work that entailed reading and other editorial duties. Special thanks go to each of the translators whose versions have been chosen for this edition. Their meticulous labor has opened up the borders of Mexico's literary landscape to other frontiers.

The result is a symphony in twenty movements, where the traditional musical rhythms of the *son* coincide, in all their geographic flavor, with the silence that the ghosts of our dead seem to voice at night. Twenty stories by twenty writers who encompass a landscape ranging from the sun-beaten coasts, with their palm trees, to the deserts with their carpets of sand; from the old bells of pueblos in the hills at dawn, to mountains that

JORGE F. HERNÁNDEZ

resemble snowy shadows on the outskirts of the greatest city in the world. Twenty stories that cannot be summarized in brief paragraphs that, in the end, would cut off the magic of their inspiration and the surprise of their respective endings; but that, as a whole, are presented here in the form of Mexico, a stain on the planet shaped like a diverse cornucopia against a blue background. The reader of these stories will feel like someone who hears the word *bougainvillea* for the first time to describe the purple mantle that hangs over an adobe wall; or tastes the juicy, yellow flesh of a mango for the first time, or the spicy, black enigma of mole sauce, or the fresh earth flavor of red Jamaica water. Like someone who strolls among millions through the middle of Mexico City, or crosses a watercolor landscape where a few figures can just barely be made out on the horizon. Like someone who hears the testimony of a man killed by injustice, or witnesses the hallucination of a writer who knows he's being read at the exact same time he writes the words down on paper.

When someone claims in English that he will make a long story short, it's understood that the story in question is actually a long one and that—for reasons of time, breath, or place—one must be brief in order to narrate it. When in Spanish, we announce that we will be brief *para no hacer el cuento largo*, it doesn't matter whether the tale in question is long or not. Rather, what really matters is the brevity with which a story can be told; the short impression that allows us to take in any landscape at a single glance; or the few words we need to share to keep a face from blurring into anonymity, to keep our stories from being lost into oblivion.

Translated by Tanya Huntington

THE FANTASTIC UNREAL

My Life with the Wave

Octavio Paz

When I left that sea, a wave moved ahead of the others. She was tall and light. In spite of the shouts of the others who grabbed her by her floating skirts, she clutched my arm and went leaping off with me. I didn't want to say anything to her, because it hurt me to shame her in front of her friends. Besides, the furious stares of the larger waves paralyzed me. When we got to town, I explained to her that it was impossible, that life in the city was not what she had been able to imagine with all the ingenuousness of a wave that had never left the sea. She watched me gravely: No, her decision was made. She couldn't go back. I tried sweetness, harshness, irony. She cried, screamed, hugged, threatened. I had to apologize.

The next day my troubles began. How could we get on the train without being seen by the conductor, the passengers, the police? It's true the rules say nothing in respect to the transport of waves on the railroad, but this very reserve was an indication of the severity with which our act would be judged. After much thought I arrived at the station an hour before departure, took my seat, and, when no one was looking, emptied the tank of the drinking fountain; then, carefully, I poured in my friend.

The first incident arose when the children of a couple nearby loudly declared their thirst. I blocked their way and promised them refreshments and lemonade. They were at the verge of accepting when another thirsty passenger approached. I was about to invite her too, but the stare of her companion stopped me short. The lady took a paper cup, approached the tank, and turned the faucet. Her cup was barely half full when I leaped between the woman and my friend. She looked at me in astonishment. While I apologized, one of the children turned the faucet again. I closed it violently. The lady brought the cup to her lips:

"Agh, this water is salty."

The boy echoed her. Various passengers rose. The husband called the conductor:

"This man put salt in the water."

The conductor called the inspector:

"So, you've placed substances in the water?"

The inspector called the police:

"So, you've poisoned the water?"

The police in turn called the captain:

"So, you're the poisoner?"

The captain called three agents. The agents took me to an empty car, amidst the stares and whispers of the passengers. At the next station they took me off and pushed and dragged me to jail. For days no one spoke to me, except during the long interrogations. No one believed me when I explained my story, not even the jailer, who shook his head, saying: "The case is grave, truly grave. You weren't trying to poison children?"

One day they brought me before the magistrate. "Your case is difficult," he repeated, "I will assign you to the penal judge."

A year passed. Finally they tried me. As there were no victims, my sentence was light. After a short time, my day of freedom arrived.

The warden called me in:

"Well, now you're free. You were lucky. Lucky there were no victims. But don't let it happen again, because the next time you'll really pay for it . . . "

And he stared at me with the same solemn stare with which everyone watched me.

That same afternoon I took the train and, after hours of uncomfortable traveling, arrived in Mexico City. I took a cab home. At the door of my apartment I heard laughter and singing. I felt a pain in my chest, like the smack of a wave of surprise when surprise smacks us in the chest: my friend was there, singing and laughing as always.

"How did you get back?"

"Easy: on the train. Someone, after making sure that I was only salt water, poured me into the engine. It was a rough trip: soon I was a white plume of vapor, then I fell in a fine rain on the machine. I thinned out a lot. I lost many drops."

Her presence changed my life. The house of dark corridors and dusty furniture was filled with air, with sun, with green and blue reflections, a numerous and happy populace of reverberations and echoes. How many waves one wave is, and how it can create a beach or rock or jetty out of a wall, a chest, a forehead that it crowns with foam! Even the abandoned corners, the abject corners of dust and debris were touched by her light hands. Everything began to laugh and everywhere white teeth shone. The sun entered the old rooms with pleasure and stayed for hours when it should have left the other houses, the district, the city, the country. And some nights, very late, the scandalized stars would watch it sneak out of my house.

Love was a game, a perpetual creation. Everything was beach, sand, a bed with sheets that were always fresh. If I embraced her, she would swell with pride, incredibly tall like the liquid stalk of a poplar, and soon that thinness would flower into a fountain of white feathers, into a plume of laughs that fell over my head and back and covered me with whiteness. Or she would stretch out in front of me, infinite as the horizon, until I too became horizon and silence. Full and sinuous, she would envelop me like music or some giant lips. Her presence was a going and coming of caresses, of murmurs, of kisses. Plunging into her waters, I would be drenched to the socks and then, in the wink of an eye, find myself high above, at a dizzying height, mysteriously suspended, to fall like a stone, and feel myself gently deposited on dry land, like a feather. Nothing is comparable to sleeping rocked in those waters, unless it is waking pounded by a thousand happy light lashes, by a thousand assaults that withdraw laughing.

But I never reached the center of her being. I never touched the nakedness of pain and of death. Perhaps it does not exist in waves, that secret place that renders a woman vulnerable and mortal, that electric button where everything interlocks, twitches, straightens out, and then swoons. Her sensibility, like that of women, spread in ripples, only they weren't concentric ripples, but rather eccentric ones that spread further each time, until they touched other galaxies. To love her was to extend to remote contacts, to vibrate with far-off stars we never suspect. But her center . . . no, she had no center, just an emptiness like a whirlwind that sucked me in and smothered me.

Stretched out side by side, we exchanged confidences, whispers, smiles. Curled up, she fell on my chest and unfolded there like a vegetation of murmurs. She sang in my ear, a little seashell. She became humble and transparent, clutching my feet like a small animal, calm water. She was so clear I could read all of her thoughts. On certain nights her skin was covered with phosphorescence and to embrace her was to embrace a piece of night tattooed with fire. But she also became black and bitter.

At unexpected hours she roared, moaned, twisted. Her groans woke the neighbors. Upon hearing her, the sea wind would scratch at the door of the house or rave in a loud voice on the roof. Cloudy days irritated her; she broke furniture, said foul words, covered me with insults and gray and greenish foam. She spat, cried, swore, prophesied. Subject to the moon, the stars, the influence of the light of other worlds, she changed her moods and appearance in a way that I thought fantastic, but was as fatal as the tide.

She began to complain of solitude. I filled the house with shells and conches, with small sailboats that in her days of fury she shipwrecked (along with the others, laden with images, that each night left my forehead and sunk in her ferocious or gentle whirlwinds). How many little treasures were lost in that time! But my boats and the silent song of the shells were not enough. I had to install a colony of fish in the house. It was not without jealousy that I watched them swimming in my friend, caressing her breasts, sleeping between her legs, adorning her hair with little flashes of color.

Among those fish there were a few particularly repulsive and ferocious ones, little tigers from the aquarium with large fixed eyes and jagged and bloodthirsty mouths. I don't know by what aberration my friend delighted in playing with them, shamelessly showing them a preference whose significance I prefer to ignore. She passed long hours confined with those horrible creatures. One day I couldn't stand it any more; I flung open the door and threw myself on them. Agile and ghostly, they slipped between my hands while she laughed and pounded me until I fell. I thought I was drowning, and when I was purple and at the point of death, she deposited me on the bank and began to kiss me, saying I don't know what things. I felt very weak, fatigued and humiliated. And at the same time her voluptuousness made me close my eyes because her voice was sweet and she spoke to me of the delicious death of the drowned. When I came to my senses, I began to fear and hate her.

I had neglected my affairs. Now I began to visit friends and renew old and dear relations. I met an old girlfriend. Making her swear to keep my secret, I told her of my life with the wave. Nothing moves women as much as the possibility of saving a man. My redeemer employed all of her arts, but what could a woman, master of a limited number of souls and bodies, do, faced with my friend who was always changing—and always identical to herself in her incessant metamorphoses.

Winter came. The sky turned gray. Fog fell on the city. A frozen drizzle rained. My friend screamed every night. During the day she isolated herself, quiet and sinister, stuttering a single syllable, like an old woman who mutters in a corner. She became cold; to sleep with her was to shiver all night and to feel, little by little, the blood, bones, and thoughts freeze. She turned deep, impenetrable, restless. I left frequently, and my absences were more prolonged each time. She, in her corner, endlessly howled. With teeth like steel and a corrosive tongue she gnawed the walls, crumbled them. She passed the nights in mourning, reproaching me. She had nightmares, deliriums of the sun, of burning beaches. She dreamt of the pole and of changing into a great block of ice, sailing beneath black skies on nights as long as months. She insulted me. She cursed and laughed, filled the house with guffaws and phantoms. She summoned blind, quick, and blunt monsters from the deep. Charged with electricity, she carbonized everything she touched. Full of acid, she dissolved whatever she brushed against. Her sweet arms became knotty cords that strangled me. And her body, greenish and elastic, was an implacable whip that lashed and lashed. I fled. The horrible fish laughed with their ferocious grins.

There in the mountains, among the tall pines and the precipices, I breathed the cold thin air like a thought of freedom. I returned at the end of a month. I had decided. It had been so cold that over the marble of the chimney, next to the extinct fire, I found a statue of ice. I was unmoved by her wearisome beauty. I put her in a big canvas sack and went out into the streets with the sleeper on my shoulders. In a restaurant in the outskirts I sold her to a waiter friend, who immediately began to chop her into little pieces, which he carefully deposited in the buckets where bottles are chilled.

Translated by Eliot Weinberger

Chac-Mool

CARLOS FUENTES

It was only recently that Filiberto drowned in Acapulco. It happened during Easter Week. Even though he'd been fired from his government job, Filiberto couldn't resist the bureaucratic temptation to make his annual pilgrimage to the small German hotel, to eat sauerkraut sweetened by the sweat of the tropical cuisine, dance away Holy Saturday on La Quebrada, and feel he was one of the "beautiful people" in the dim anonymity of dusk on Hornos Beach. Of course we all knew he'd been a good swimmer when he was young, but now, at forty, and the shape he was in, to try to swim that distance, at midnight! Frau Müller wouldn't allow a wake in her hotel—steady client or not; just the opposite, she held a dance on her stifling little terrace while Filiberto, very pale in his coffin, awaited the departure of the first morning bus from the terminal, spending the first night of his new life surrounded by crates and parcels. When I arrived, early in the morning, to supervise the loading of the casket, I found Filiberto buried beneath a mound of coconuts; the driver wanted to get him in the luggage compartment as quickly as possible, covered with canvas in order not to upset the passengers and to avoid bad luck on the trip.

When we left Acapulco there was still a good breeze. Near Tierra Colorada it began to get hot and bright. As I was eating my breakfast eggs and sausage, I had opened Filiberto's satchel, collected the day before along with his other personal belongings from the Müllers' hotel. Two hundred pesos. An old newspaper; expired lottery tickets; a one-way ticket to Acapulco —one way?—and a cheap notebook with graph-paper pages and marbleized-paper binding.

On the bus I ventured to read it, in spite of the sharp curves, the stench of vomit, and a certain natural feeling of respect for the private life of a deceased friend. It should be a record—yes, it began that way—of our daily office routine; maybe I'd find out what caused him to neglect his duties, why he'd written memoranda without rhyme or reason or any authorization. The reasons, in short, for his being fired, his seniority ignored, and his pension lost.

"Today I went to see about my pension. Lawyer extremely pleasant. I was so happy when I left that I decided to blow five pesos at a café. The same café we used to go to when we were young and where I never go now because it reminds me that I lived better at twenty than I do at forty. We were all equals then, energetically discouraging any unfavorable remarks about our classmates. In fact, we'd open fire on anyone in the house who so much as mentioned inferior background or lack of elegance. I knew that many of us (perhaps those of most humble origin) would go far, and that here in school we were forging lasting friendships: together we would brave the stormy seas of life. But it didn't work out that way. Someone didn't follow the rules. Many of the lowly were left behind, though some climbed higher even than we could have predicted in those high-spirited, affable get-togethers. Some who seemed to have the most promise got stuck somewhere along the way, cut down in some extra-curricular activity, isolated by an invisible chasm from those who'd triumphed and those who'd gone nowhere at all. Today, after all this time, I again sat in the chairs—remodeled, as well as the soda fountain, a kind of barricade against invasion—and pretended to read some business papers. I saw many of the old faces, amnesiac, changed in the neon light, prosperous. Like the café, which I barely recognized, along with the city itself, they'd been chipping away at a pace different from my own. No, they didn't recognize me now, or didn't want to. At most, one or two clapped a quick, fat hand on my shoulder. So long, old friend, how's it been going? Between us stretched the eighteen holes of the country club. I buried myself in my papers. The years of my dreams, the optimistic predictions, filed before my eyes, along with the obstacles that had kept me from achieving them. I felt frustrated that I couldn't dig my fingers into the past and put together the pieces of some long-forgotten puzzle. But one's toy chest is a part of the past, and when all's said and done, who knows where his lead soldiers went, his helmets and wooden swords. The make-believe we loved so much was only that, make-believe. Still, I'd been diligent, disciplined, devoted to duty. Wasn't that enough? Was it too much? Often, I was assaulted by the recollection of Rilke: the great reward for the adventure of youth is death; we should die young, taking all our secrets with us. Today I wouldn't be looking back at a city of salt. Five pesos? Two pesos tip."

"In addition to his passion for corporate law, Pepe likes to theorize. He saw me coming out of the cathedral, and we walked together toward the National Palace. He's not a believer, but he's not content to stop at that: within half a block he had to propose a theory. If I weren't a Mexican, I wouldn't worship Christ, and 'No, look, it's obvious. The Spanish arrive and say, *Adore this God who died a bloody death nailed to a cross with a bleeding wound in his side. Sacrificed. Made an offering.* What could be

CHAC-MOOL

more natural than to accept something so close to your own ritual, your own life . . . ? Imagine, on the other hand, if Mexico had been conquered by Buddhists or Moslems. It's not conceivable that our Indians would have worshipped some person who died of indigestion. But a God that's not only sacrificed for you but has his heart torn out, God Almighty, checkmate to Huitzilopochtli![1] Christianity, with its emotion, its bloody sacrifice and ritual, becomes a natural and novel extension of the native religion. The qualities of charity, love, and turn-the-other-cheek, however, are rejected. And that's what Mexico is all about: you have to kill a man in order to believe in him.'

"Pepe knew that ever since I was young I've been mad for certain pieces of Mexican Indian art. I collect small statues, idols, pots. I spend my weekends in Tlaxcala,[2] or in Teotihuacán.[3] That may be why he likes to relate to indigenous themes all the theories he concocts for me. Pepe knows that I've been looking for a reasonable replica of the Chac-Mool[4] for a long time, and today he told me about a little shop in the flea market of La Lagunilla where they're selling one, apparently at a good price. I'll go Sunday.

"A joker put red coloring in the office water cooler, naturally interrupting our duties. I had to report him to the direc-

---

[1] *Huitzilopochtli*: Aztec god of war and the sun whose name means "blue hummingbird on the left (or south)," traditionally said to have guided the Aztecs in migration from mythical Aztlán to the Valley of Mexico. He required the sacrifice of human hearts to appease him.

[2] *Tlaxcala*: capital city of Tlaxcala state in central Mexico, historically prominent for remaining unconquered by the Aztecs.

[3] *Teotihuacán*: monumental archaeological site northeast of Mexico City containing some of the largest pre-Columbian pyramids.

[4] *Chac-Mool*: any pre-Columbian stone statue depicting a reclining figure with knees drawn up, head to one side, and a tray lying across the stomach. The statue is typically found in ritual environments associated with a rain god.

tor, who simply thought it was funny. So all day the bastard's been going around making fun of me, with cracks about water. Motherfu . . . "

"Today, Sunday, I had time to go out to La Lagunilla. I found the Chac-Mool in the cheap little shop Pepe had told me about. It's a marvelous piece, life-size, and though the dealer assures me it's an original, I question it, the stone is nothing out of the ordinary, but that doesn't diminish the elegance of the composition, or its massiveness. The rascal has smeared tomato ketchup on the belly to convince the tourists of its bloody authenticity.

"Moving the piece to my house cost more than the purchase price. But it's here now, temporarily in the cellar while I reorganize my collection to make room for it. These figures demand a vertical and burning-hot sun; that was their natural element. The effect is lost in the darkness of the cellar, where it's simply another lifeless mass and its grimace seems to reproach me for denying it light. The dealer had a spotlight focused directly on the sculpture, highlighting all the planes and lending a more amiable expression to my Chac-Mool. I must follow his example."

"I awoke to find the pipes had burst. Somehow, I'd carelessly left the water running in the kitchen; it flooded the floor and poured into the cellar before I'd noticed it. The dampness didn't damage the Chac-Mool, but my suitcases suffered; everything has to happen on a weekday. I was late to work."

"At last they came to fix the plumbing. Suitcases ruined. There's slime on the base of the Chac-Mool."

"I awakened at one; I'd heard a terrible moan. I thought it might be burglars. Purely imaginary."

"The moaning at night continues. I don't know where it's coming from, but it makes me nervous. To top it all off, the pipes burst again, and the rains have seeped through the foundation and flooded the cellar."

"Plumber still hasn't come; I'm desperate. As far as the city water department's concerned, the less said the better. This is the first time the runoff from the rains has drained into my cellar instead of the storm sewers. The moaning's stopped. An even trade?"

"They pumped out the cellar. The Chac-Mool is covered with slime, it makes him look grotesque; the whole sculpture seems to be suffering from a kind of green erysipelas, with the exception of the eyes. I'll scrape off the moss Sunday. Pepe suggested I move to an apartment on an upper floor, to prevent any more of these aquatic tragedies. But I can't leave my house; it's obviously more than I need, a little gloomy in its turn-of-the-century style, but it's the only inheritance, the only memory, I have left of my parents. I don't know how I'd feel if I saw a soda fountain with a jukebox in the cellar and an interior decorator's shop on the ground floor."

"Used a trowel to scrape the Chac-Mool. The moss now seemed almost a part of the stone; it took more than an hour and it was six in the evening before I finished. I couldn't see anything in the darkness, but I ran my hand over the outlines of the stone. With every stroke, the stone seemed to become softer. I couldn't believe it; it felt like dough. That dealer in La Lagunilla has really swindled me. His 'pre-Columbian sculpture' is nothing but plaster, and the dampness is ruining it. I've covered it with some rags and will bring it upstairs tomorrow before it dissolves completely."

"The rags are on the floor. Incredible. Again I felt the Chac-Mool. It's firm, but not stone. I don't want to write this: the texture of the torso feels a little like flesh; I press it like rubber, and feel something coursing through that recumbent figure . . . I went down again later at night. No doubt about it: the Chac-Mool has hair on its arms."

"This kind of thing has never happened to me before. I fouled up my work in the office: I sent out a payment that hadn't been authorized, and the director had to call it to my attention. I think I may even have been rude to my co-workers. I'm going to have to see a doctor, find out whether it's my imagination, whether I'm delirious, or what . . . and get rid of that damned Chac-Mool."

Up to this point I recognized Filiberto's hand, the large, rounded letters I'd seen on so many memoranda and forms. The entry for August 25 seemed to have been written by a different person. At times it was the writing of a child, each letter laboriously separated; other times, nervous, trailing into illegibility. Three days are blank, and then the narrative continues:

"It's all so natural, though normally we believe only in what's real . . . but this is real, more real than anything I've ever known. A water cooler is real, more than real, because we fully realize its existence, or being, when some joker puts something in the water to turn it red . . . An ephemeral smoke ring is real, a grotesque image in a fun-house mirror is real; aren't all deaths, present and forgotten, real . . . ? If a man passes through paradise in a dream, and is handed a flower as proof of having been there, and if when he awakens he finds this flower in his hand . . . then . . . ? Reality: one day it was shattered into a thousand pieces, its head rolled in one direction and its tail in another, and all we have is one of the pieces from the gigantic body. A free and fictitious ocean, real only when it is imprisoned in a seashell. Until three days ago, my reality was of such a degree it would be erased today; it was reflex action, routine, memory, carapace. And then, like the earth that one day trembles to remind us of its power, of the death to come, recriminating against me for having turned my back on life, an orphaned reality we always knew was there presents itself, jolting us in order to become living present. Again I believed it to be imagination: the Chac-Mool, soft and elegant, had changed color overnight; yellow, almost golden, it seemed to suggest it was a god, at ease now, the knees more relaxed than before, the smile more benevolent. And yesterday, finally, I awakened with a start, with the frightening certainty that two creatures are breathing in the night, that in the darkness there beats a pulse in addition to one's own. Yes, I heard footsteps on the stairway. Nightmare. Go back to sleep. I don't know how long I feigned sleep. When I opened my eyes again, it still was not dawn. The room smelled of horror, of incense and blood. In the darkness, I gazed about the bedroom until my eyes found two points of flickering, cruel yellow light.

"Scarcely breathing, I turned on the light.

"There was the Chac-Mool, standing erect, smiling, ocher-colored except for the flesh-red belly. I was paralyzed by the two tiny, almost crossed eyes set close to the wedge-shaped nose. The lower teeth closed tightly on the upper lip; only the glimmer from the squarish helmet on the abnormally large head betrayed any sign of life. Chac-Mool moved toward my bed; then it began to rain."

I remember that it was at the end of August that Filiberto had been fired from his job, with a public condemnation by the director, amid rumors of madness and even theft. I didn't believe it. I did see some wild memoranda, one asking the secretary of the department whether water had an odor; another, offering his services to the Department of Water Resources to make it rain in the desert. I couldn't explain it. I thought the exceptionally heavy rains of that summer had affected him. Or that living in that ancient mansion with half the rooms locked and thick with dust, without any servants or family life, had finally deranged him. The following entries are for the end of September:

"Chac-Mool can be pleasant enough when he wishes . . . the gurgling of enchanted water . . . He knows wonderful stories about the monsoons, the equatorial rains, the scourge of the deserts; the genealogy of every plant engendered by his mythic paternity: the willow, his wayward daughter; the lotus, his favorite child; the cactus, his mother-in-law. What I can't bear is the odor, the nonhuman odor, emanating from flesh that isn't flesh, from sandals that shriek their antiquity. Laughing stridently, the Chac-Mool recounts how he was discovered by Le Plongeon and brought into physical contact with men of other gods. His spirit had survived quite peacefully in water vessels and storms; his stone was another matter, and to have dragged him from his hiding place was unnatural and cruel. I think the Chac-Mool will never forgive that. He savors the imminence of the aesthetic.

"I've had to provide him with pumice stone to clean the belly the dealer smeared with ketchup when he thought he was Aztec. He didn't seem to like my question about his relation to Tlaloc, and when he becomes angry his teeth, repulsive enough in themselves, glitter and grow pointed. The first days he slept in the cellar; since yesterday, in my bed."

"The dry season has begun. Last night, from the living room where I'm sleeping now, I heard the same hoarse moans I'd heard in the beginning, followed by a terrible racket. I went upstairs and peered into the bedroom: the Chac-Mool was breaking the lamps and furniture; he sprang toward the door with outstretched bleeding hands, and I was barely able to slam the door and run to hide in the bathroom. Later he came downstairs, panting and begging for water. He leaves the faucets running all day; there's not a dry spot in the house. I have to sleep wrapped in blankets, and I've asked him please to let the living room dry out."*

"The Chac-Mool flooded the living room today. Exasperated, I told him I was going to return him to La Lagunilla. His laughter—so frighteningly different from the laugh of any man or animal—was as terrible as the blow from that heavily braceleted arm. I have to admit it: I am his prisoner. My original plan was quite different. I was going to play with the Chac-Mool the way you play with a toy; this may have been an extension of the security of childhood. But—who said it?— the fruit of childhood is consumed by the years, and I hadn't seen that. He's taken my clothes, and when the green moss

* Filiberto does not say in what language he communicated with the Chac-Mool.

begins to sprout, he covers himself in my bathrobes. The Chac-Mool is accustomed to obedience, always; I, who have never had cause to command, can only submit. Until it rains— what happened to his magic power?—he will be choleric and irritable."

"Today I discovered that the Chac-Mool leaves the house at night. Always, as it grows dark, he sings a shrill and ancient tune, older than song itself. Then everything is quiet. I knocked several times at the door, and when he didn't answer I dared enter. The bedroom, which I hadn't seen since the day the statue tried to attack me, is a ruin; the odor of incense and blood that permeates the entire house is particularly concentrated here. And I discovered bones behind the door, dog and rat and cat bones. This is what the Chac-Mool steals in the night for nourishment. This explains the hideous barking every morning."

"February, dry. Chac-Mool watches every move I make; he made me telephone a restaurant and ask them to deliver chicken and rice every day. But what I took from the office is about to run out. So the inevitable happened: on the first they cut off the water and lights for nonpayment. But Chac has discovered a public fountain two blocks from the house; I make ten or twelve trips a day for water while he watches me from the roof. He says that if I try to run away he will strike me dead in my tracks; he is also the God of Lightning. What he doesn't realize is that I know about his nighttime forays. Since we don't have any electricity, I have to go to bed about eight. I should be used to the Chac-Mool by now, but just a moment ago, when I ran into him on the stairway, I touched his icy arms, the scales of his renewed skin, and I wanted to scream.

"If it doesn't rain soon, the Chac-Mool will return to stone. I've noticed his recent difficulty in moving; sometimes he lies for hours, paralyzed, and almost seems an idol again. But this repose merely gives him new strength to abuse me, to claw at me as if he could extract liquid from my flesh. We don't have the amiable intervals any more, when he used to tell me old tales; instead, I seem to notice a heightened resentment. There have been other indications that set me thinking: my wine cellar is diminishing; he likes to stroke the silk of my bathrobes; he wants me to bring a servant girl to the house; he has made me teach him how to use soap and lotions. I believe the Chac-Mool is falling into human temptations; now I see in the face that once seemed eternal something that is merely old. This may be my salvation: if the Chac becomes human, it's possible that all the centuries of his life will accumulate in an instant and he will die in a flash of lightning. But this might also cause my death: the Chac won't want me to witness his downfall; he may decide to kill me.

"I plan to take advantage tonight of Chac's nightly excursion to flee. I will go to Acapulco; I'll see if I can't find a job, and await the death of the Chac-Mool. Yes, it will be soon; his hair is gray, his face bloated. I need to get some sun, to swim, to regain my strength. I have four hundred pesos left. I'll go to the Müllers' hotel, it's cheap and comfortable. Let Chac-Mool take over the whole place; we'll see how long he lasts without my pails of water."

Filiberto's diary ends here. I didn't want to think about what he'd written; I slept as far as Cuernavaca. From there to Mexico City I tried to make some sense out of the account, to attribute it to overwork, or some psychological disturbance, by the time we reached the terminal at nine in the evening, I still hadn't accepted the fact of my friend's madness. I hired a truck to carry the coffin to Filiberto's house, where I would arrange for his burial.

Before I could insert the key in the lock, the door opened. A yellow-skinned Indian in a smoking jacket and ascot stood in the doorway. He couldn't have been more repulsive; he smelled of cheap cologne; he'd tried to cover his wrinkles with thick powder, his mouth was clumsily smeared with lipstick, and his hair appeared to be dyed.

"I'm sorry . . . I didn't know that Filiberto had . . . "

"No matter. I know all about it. Tell the men to carry the body down to the cellar."

Translated by Margaret Sayers Peden

History According to Pao Cheng

Salvador Elizondo

On a summer day, over thirty-five hundred years ago, the philosopher Pao Cheng[1] sat at the edge of a stream to foresee his
destiny on the shell of a tortoise. The heat and the murmuring
of the water, however, soon drove his thoughts astray, and slowly
forgetting the stains on the tortoise shell, Pao Cheng began to
infer the history of the world from that moment on. "As the
ripples of this brook, so time flows. This small channel grows
as it runs, soon to become rushing water, leading off to sea,
crossing the ocean, rising as steam towards the clouds, and
again falling over the mountain with the rain, finally descend-
ing, once again converted in the same stream . . . " This was,
more or less, the course of his thoughts and thus, once his
intuition had discovered the roundness of Earth, its movement
round the Sun, the course followed by all other astronomical
bodies, the very rotation of the galaxy and the world itself,
"Bah!" he exclaimed, "These thoughts drive me away from the
Land of Han and his people, who are the immobile center
and axis around which all humanities that inhabit it turn . . . "
And, thinking once again about mankind, Pao Cheng pondered history. He deciphered, as if they had been written

[1] *Pao Cheng*: a legendary Sung Dynasty judge who put the scholar Chen
Shih-mei on trial for attempted murder. Chen Shih-mei tried to kill his
wife and children in order to marry into the royal family.

across the tortoise shell, the great events of the future, the wars, the migrations, the plagues and epic feats of all men and lands throughout several millennia. Before the eyes of his imagination great nations fell and small ones were born, later to become large and powerful, only to be defeated in turn. All the races of man also emerged and the cities they inhabited rose majestically in an instant, then tumbled down to mingle with the rabble and ruins of countless generations. One city among all those that existed in the future imagined by Pao Cheng forcefully caught his attention and his wandering thoughts became more precise concerning all the details that composed that city, as if an enigma relating to his person were contained within. He sharpened his inner vision and tried to penetrate within the crevices of that yet-to-be-created topography. The force of his imagination was such that he felt himself walking through those streets, raising his bewildered eyes towards the grandeur of the construction and beauty of the monuments. For a long while Pao Cheng wandered in that city, blending in among men attired in strange clothing, speaking in a very slow, incomprehensible tongue, until he suddenly stopped before a house with a façade where the indecipherable signs of a mystery that irresistibly drew him were inscribed. Through one of the windows he could envision a man, writing. At that precise moment, Pao Cheng felt that a question intimately concerning him was being pondered then and there. He closed his eyes, and with the tip of his outstretched fingers, caressed his forehead pearled with sweat, trying to penetrate with his thoughts the room where the man was writing. He arose, flying over the pavement, and his imagination crossed the open windowsill that allowed a fresh gust of air to rustle the sheets of paper, lying upon the table, filled with incomprehensible characters. Pao Cheng cautiously approached the man and looked over his shoulder, holding his breath so his presence would go unnoticed. The man would not have noticed him, for he seemed absorbed in his task of covering those sheets of paper with signs, whose contents still escaped Pao Cheng's comprehension. Once in a while the man would stop and gaze pensively beyond the window, inhaling from a small white cylinder that burned on one end and blowing out a puff of bluish smoke from his mouth and nostrils, then writing once again. Pao Cheng saw the finished pages piled in disarray on one end of the table and as he gradually deciphered the meaning of the words written on them, his face began to cloud and a chill of terror ran through his body, as if a poisonous snake were creeping up his spine. "This man is writing a story," he said to himself. Pao Cheng read once again the words written on the pages. "The story's title is *History According to Pao Cheng*, and it's about a philosopher of ancient times who one day sat at the edge of a stream and began to ponder . . . Then I am but a memory of this man, and if this man should forget me, I shall die! . . . "

The man, as soon as he had written " . . . if this man should forget me, I shall die," lifted his pen, inhaled from his cigarette again and as he allowed the smoke to escape from his mouth, shadows covered his gaze as if a cloud filled with rain had passed before him. He understood, at that moment, that he had condemned himself forever, for all eternity, to continue writing the story of Pao Cheng, for if his character were forgotten and perished, he—who was nothing more than a thought of Pao Cheng's—would also disappear.

Translated by Jorge F. Hernández

The Night of Margaret Rose

FRANCISCO TARIO

The letter, written a tad less than illegibly, read:

> X.X. Esq.
> 97 Cromwell Road
> London S.W. 7

> Margaret Lane Rose, British, age twenty-eight, married to a Yankee multimillionaire, invites you most cordially to play chess with her this Saturday evening.

And at the bottom, in block letters, figured a series of highly detailed instructions regarding the exact location of the estate at Brighton's Way, some twenty-five kilometers off the coast.

In my vague recollection, Margaret Lane Rose boiled down to nothing more than this: a dreadfully pale, ethereal slip of a girl dressed in green, who played chess admirably.

Digging deeper into my memory, I later was able, however, to reconstruct certain particulars.

I'd made her acquaintance in Rome—by virtue of what ordinary incident, I can't quite seem to place—at Saint Sebastian's church, moments before our descent into the catacombs. She was accompanied, I believe, by a French governess who was farsighted, or something of the sort. A slip of a girl who must have been seventeen or eighteen years old at the time. In fact, I recall her figure, not far ahead in the underground grotto, perfectly well. She held a mysterious candle, whose blue—or gray—glow was trembling against her black hair, like a lick of fire over a wet surface. I found the contrast between the two characters who preceded me to be indescribably telling: the guide—a Carmelite, with curly locks and aquiline nose—and that quiet, bashful, spiritual damsel who often sighed as she picked her way between the open tombs and scattered skulls.

We met on three other occasions. Once, fortuitously, at the Roman Forum, and then, by mutual agreement, at her own hotel —the London Hotel?—chaperoned by her relatives. (I can't remember how many of them there were, probably three). During our last two encounters, I was able to attest to the young woman's extraordinary chess playing abilities, which naturally impressed me. I don't believe I won a single match.

Just as we were about to say farewell that final night—they were setting sail from Naples shortly—I remember what she said to me quite clearly: "Soon, very soon, Mr X, you shall forget Margaret Rose . . . "

None of this has any real importance, and doubtless I would have forgotten all about it, if not for what happened next.

There we were in the hotel reading room, the two of us seated at a small, square table, with my king in checkmate, when the girl stretched her hand out over the board and added, contritely:

"Why are people so ungrateful, Mr X?"

I concocted some sort of false, idiotic reasoning, in hopes of dissuading her from the actual, bitter truth. But contrary to what one might expect, she reacted in a most unusual way. She withdrew her arm slowly, turned frighteningly pale, fixed her feverish gaze upon me, and babbled in the precise tone of, shall we say, a sleepwalker:

"Yes, all right, then. We shan't ever see each other again . . . "

After which she immediately covered her face with her hands and began to sob uncontrollably.

The French governess appeared—and here we come to the strangest part of the affair. Far from showing surprise or alarm, she silently drew near and, offering her hand, helped the young woman to her feet, then proceeded to dry her tears, as you would a small child's. After that, addressing me with the utmost solemnity, she implored:

"If you'll excuse us, sir. I'm sure you understand."

I watched as they moved off towards the vestibule. I never saw Miss Margaret Rose again.

I went back to America, and twenty days after my arrival in New York, I unexpectedly received a postcard from London. Margaret Rose sent her regards, "in enormous gratitude for the wonderful times we'd had in Italy."

And now, this strange and unexpected missive. The first news I've had from her since then.

How unpredictable and sensational life can be, after all!

Fifty years old now, with white hair, my spirit worn down by endless physical and moral complaints, I find enormous satisfaction in finding that there are reserves of optimism and vigor still intact beneath these bones. It's uncommon, to say the least, for a man in my condition to have found something truly interesting or attractive in the simple, melancholy things that surround us. Actual beauty can be exaggerated by love, or mint physical condition, or an eagerness for all those unknown pleasures. A warm, blue day exalts us. A round, clean moon moves us. We feel the ebb and flow of tides as if they circulated in our bloodstream. Music wrings tears from us, or cries of sense-less joy. Alcohol stirs our deepest instincts. We find nighttime pleasing because it's dark and propitious; daytime, because it's bright and merry. And those vibrating muscles of ours, that continuous galloping of our hearts, all that insatiable hunger derived from our physical and intellectual potential, cloak real-ity in an opulent attire of vitality, transparency, and ardor. An attire that, sadly enough, gradually and inopportunely fades with the passage of time, until finally, inexorably, like a beauti-ful afternoon that ends, or an earthenware pot that breaks, we find ourselves surrounded by starvation, coldness, and terrify-ing shadows.

Through the small window of the train compartment, I now contemplate fields transported by the fecundity of spring. A sweet, unsteady breeze sways the reeds, the living stems of flowers, the iridescent branches of trees, the white clothing hung out to dry on the stone walls of the corrals. Cattle graze or drink, their hooves submerged in the wet core of grass. Swift, playful swallows pass by while calling raucously. Streams quiver, and their tremor is divinely musical and tender. The blue—or brown—smoke from the coal stretches high up, high beneath the metallic heavens, breaking into pieces—a jumble of incon-sistent clouds, inevitably absorbed by that solemn, luminous vastness.

And I sustain the impression, by virtue of these unremark-able and constantly repeating events, of an impatience similar to that of a thirsty man who finds himself before a clear, gur-gling spring. Like a true adolescent, or like one who's never ventured beyond the boundaries of his shire, I keep a close eye on everything that happens around me. Yet it would be logical, after having gone halfway around the world, having witnessed —and also suffered—relatively painful events, if this English countryside, so smooth, so unsubstantial, so phlegmatic, were to lead me to unfold my newspaper and divert my gaze from that which it has contemplated countless times. Far from it, though: I watch the sun set, set there on the horizon, and within me also, something descends, darkens, falls silent, and I fear—well, it had to happen someday—that I too shall die someday.

As always, this concept of the inevitable or the light that dies out, dampens my spirits while my thoughts become impenetrable.

So I draw the curtains and, inside my solitary compartment on the express, give myself over to another genre of reflection.

Margaret Rose . . . Margaret Rose . . . How distant and obscure our encounter renders itself to me! It's as if another ten years had passed since the day I received her last letter; I can scarcely manage now to relive the most insignificant detail. Yet I've thought about nothing else over the past few days, persisting until I was able to obtain useful information from my memory. And even today I repeat, now more forcefully than ever, that the existence and proximity of such a woman seems bizarre.

Over and over again I read her impenetrable message, which I keep safe in my pocket.

Margaret Rose . . . I close my eyes to try and connect her physiognomical features, only to wind up tempestuously evoking a gesture of hers I'd forgotten completely: that of her stretching out one fine, white hand towards a chess piece, grasping it by the tip, then finally sliding it across the board in one mysteriously swift motion . . . Margaret Rose . . . a strange, unique creature, always dressed in green. I can see her now, leaning against a tree, fatigued, short of breath under the torrid Italian sun, observing all around her with a peculiar expression of thoughtlessness, or distrustfulness . . . Margaret Rose . . . now married to a Yankee multimillionaire . . .

The train shudders abruptly, noisily coming to a stop and at the very same moment, a large number of travelers cross the passageway, their meager luggage in hand.

. . . A nasty love story? An innocent, naïve, sentimental enrapture? The childish, or rather, the sickly eccentricity of a wealthy, bored young woman? A grave and urgent cry for help that I cannot give, a secret purpose that causes her great personal distress? Blackmail? Cowardly revenge, sought by one of my numerous enemies . . . ?

No sooner had I set foot on the ground than a yellowish little man approached me on the train platform and inquired after my name. Once he'd identified me, he decidedly picked up my suitcase, gesturing that I should follow him. He leads the way, I follow: we cross the waiting room, go down a few blackened steps, and arrive at a splendid carriage, drawn by a team of magnificent white horses.

Out of the pitch-black night, flickering lights appear on both sides of the road. They are few and far between, and yet in their gleam, the foliage takes on a mysterious, underwater vivaciousness. At full gallop, the horses press on through deep, uncharacteristically dark territories, whose murmuring is quite agreeable to me. There are many curves, quite pronounced at times, and I'm obliged to hold on tight to keep from flying out of the vehicle. I perceive, at almost equal intervals, the whip cracking in the air. Frogs croak in a pond that I surmise to be close by, the lamps disappear occasionally, the horses quicken their gait, while up above, a handful of insignificant stars twinkles against the dense, mauve sky.

Suddenly, the lights of a home that, at first glance, seems immense come into view over the treetops from a distance. We come to a stop outside a large gate, sections of which are covered by flowering, exuberant vines. The lights in the building go out—along with our arrival—until a single window on the top floor is left aglow. The coachman alights and I do the same, preparing to follow him. He switches an electric lamp on. For ten minutes, more or less, we skirt the enormous orchard beneath an impressive mass of foliage, gently lulled by the wind. A small, lancet door that has been embedded into a thick wall, like a crypt, seems to be our present destination. My companion sets down the suitcase, produces a key from his pocket, inserts it into the keyhole and the door gives way, but not without some resistance. Inside the yellowish, flickering lights are somewhat dim. We feel our way along a steep, spiral staircase that climbs up into the shadows. The naked walls, the total lack of furniture and a certain penetrating smell of stews and spices all alert me to the fact that we're in the servants' quarters. But there are no voices or noises to be heard, as if the house were deserted, or all of its inhabitants asleep.

Once upstairs, we cross a vast stone corridor covered by threadbare, scarlet carpeting. Another door for us to enter. A small, dark hall and then another door, on which the coachman energetically pounds. I make several attempts to give him a tip, thus signaling the end of my journey, but he refuses time and time again. In the end, he disappears with my luggage and I can distinguish the soft steps of someone approaching within the silent chamber. In effect, the door opens and I find myself face to face with Margaret Lane Rose, in person.

Margaret Rose—now I remember—exactly as I knew her ten years ago. Just as languid, just as pale, perhaps a bit more frail, and with two phenomenal, dark eyes—I don't know how I managed to forget them so easily!—and her straight, black hair, gathered at the nape of her neck.

We remain standing face to face, in silence, staring intently at one another. She ventures a smile and I, inexplicably, can find nothing appropriate to say, despite several vain attempts.

"Margaret . . . " I manage to utter laboriously at last.

So serious, so aerial, her green robe down to her ankles, she locks the door behind us and asks me to have a seat.

I choose an exceedingly soft and wide armchair, from which my torso emerges like a scraggly bush in a large trench. She sits across from me, her countenance strangely impassive. A small chess table, its pieces all laid out, separates us. A huge fire—I can't imagine why, in spring—roars in the stone chimney. The room seems immense, gives the impression of finding itself empty.

"Margaret . . . " I blurt out once more; and my voice is so distant that I'm surprised to find myself speaking. "Is this all, perhaps, a dream?"

She smiles. Her phenomenal pupils are fixed, fixed on me.

"Is this a dream?" I repeat instinctively, trying to set off once again that awful, nearly corporeal echo that slithers along the walls.

She laughs and says nothing, pleased, perhaps, by my confusion.

Indeed: with each passing moment an acute, completely undecipherable malaise gradually takes hold of me. A sensation that is most strange, neither discomfort nor anguish, neither anxiety nor shock, neither dread nor mistrust, but rather emptiness, instability, or absence. It's as if my personality, let's say, were gradually being annulled by another, intrusive personality taking its place. Much like waking from a dream, much like falling asleep . . .

"Margaret," I insist; and from the ceiling, a voice that isn't mine crashes down: "Margareeeet."

I continue:

"I've fallen prey to I know not what strange impression upon entering this place and finding myself here with you again. Forgive me! When I received your letter a few days ago, I was possessed by a fervent desire to remember, to remember freely those far-off times in Italy together. But now, seeing things in a different light, I don't know if I should perhaps reproach myself for having kept this appointment. It isn't prudent to be rash, and I believe I've been rash and then some on this particular occasion . . . "

She laughs, she laughs: her small, squared teeth show. And the laughter shakes her body, then smashes against the walls with a sound similar to that of hail striking a tin roof.

"No, what we're doing isn't prudent . . . "

She can't stop laughing, she covers her face with both hands, and I'm ready to throw myself at her to make that laughter stop once and for all.

"Are you mocking me?" I exclaim, restraining myself, but already comprehending that something far more serious and sinister lurks behind those convulsive lips.

She laughs, she laughs while she takes me in, her head tilted to one side.

"For this, Margaret Rose, for this you've brought me into your home? For this . . . ?"

Already, an unprecedented volatility has taken hold of me. I can't seem to coordinate my reflections properly, much less find a judicious way to silence the laughter that penetrates my ears, diving into the shadows of my body, crushing my nerves.

"Enough, now, that's enough, Margaret!" I plead while getting to my feet, still uncertain as to whether to move towards her. "Perhaps you find yourself fatigued, or slightly ill . . . It would be best if you took your leave and got some rest, don't you think? I promise to return whenever you like!"

And now she laughs even more scandalously, looking me up and down. She laughs, and that waterfall of laughter that threatens to never end has slightly reddened her cheeks and filled her eyes with tears. She laughs, and in the lugubrious intimacy of the chamber, that open, tense mouth is intermittently illuminated by the glow of the flames. She laughs, she laughs, as I prepare my exit, moving towards the door. Then suddenly, she falls silent. And an excessive, supernatural silence grows all around me; a silence unlike any other, making me stop short. I turn my head, fearing I'll encounter a limp body there on the carpet, and instead, I find myself before an inscrutable, cold face, absolutely still above a neck as stiff and firm as the point of a rock. We exchange mistrustful glares, frightened perhaps of ourselves. We remain thus for some time, I at the opposite end of the room. The silence hums, or is it my blood? The logs crackle. Then, mechanically, as if that strange personality I've already mentioned were controlling my muscles, now, to such an extent that any attempt to defend myself would be in vain, I spin around, retrace my steps back to the armchair, and sit down.

The silence that reins is enormous, profound, intoxicating.

But Margaret Rose throws her head back, half closes her phenomenal eyes, and muses with unhealthy languor, rhythmically moving her lips:

"That stupid laugh!"

She sighs.

"That horrible laugh, Mr X! A horrible, horrible laugh and I don't know where it springs from . . . !"

She lies there, motionless, her expression visibly sad, in complete abandonment while she lets the sweet, caressing, painful words flow.

"Horrible horrible, because at night, when everyone's asleep and no one listens, the laughter races about unleashed, striking doors that are always locked. Locked doors are horrible too, Mr X!"

I don't know how to describe the fascination emanating from her now ecstatic face.

"If an orchard is closed, you can call out apprehensively, and no one will open . . . If a door is locked, nothing can be done: just laugh and laugh, and the laughter is sheer torture. But that won't get it to open! We can leave our entrails behind, faint away or go mad, and not one single hand will push the door open . . . Don't you find that appalling, Mr X?"

Her immobility becomes more and more intense, and her gaze is lost in the invisible vault. Her words well up unnervingly, too slowly, like a venom that is lethal, albeit extraordinarily exquisite in taste.

"That damned laughter!"

Again, the unbearable silence.

Then an eerie, incomprehensibly forgotten idea illuminates my brain. An idea that hadn't given the slightest hint of its true nature, leaving me paralyzed in my seat, in a state just short of consciousness.

"Margaret Lane Rose passed away some time ago."

When? I can't seem to pin it down at this terrible moment, but the certainty of the fact leaves no room for doubt. Perhaps five, six years ago . . . How could I not clearly remember the exact moment I received the news? A newspaper at the club, a certain evening . . .

"Margaret!" I exclaim, leaping to my feet, my lips trembling irrepressibly. "Margaret! Is it true?"

My voice must have startled her, or the sweat pouring down my temples, or my assuredly diabolical expression, because her attitude has changed completely from the one she's adopted up to now. She also rises, advancing noiselessly—like a true ghost— then once she's very close to me, making me feel the warmth of her breath, she asks:

"Mr X, what's come over you? Are you not feeling well? Oh, do calm down!"

"Margaret! Margaret!" I blurt out while backing away, try- ing to avoid at all costs the slightest contact with that abomi- nable being. "Tell me the truth, you must!"

"The truth?" she smiles sadly and, to my growing amaze- ment, gently leans her head against my shoulder. "The truth, Mr X, is that I'm most unfortunate . . . "

She continues:

"You can't imagine how often I've thought of you!" and two slow, bitter tears roll down to her lips, then fall from her face and land on my shoulder. "Oh! If only that same afternoon, the earth had cracked open and everything had ended in a second . . . "

She weeps, she weeps, and both of us, standing there in the lamplight, are nothing but two absurd beings, illusions of sorts, whose presence would have melted the coldest heart on earth.

"One day, if you like, I'll make my confession to you, and you'll be horrified! How terrible, oh, how terrible and frightful it's all been!"

She looks around, suddenly restless, as if afraid that which she speaks of so desperately might present itself.

"When we emerged from the catacombs, on the last step of stairs, you offered me your hand. We were already inside the church . . . The Carmelite was waiting . . . Mademoiselle Fourni- er had lagged behind . . . I told you: 'Take me with you, for- ever, I beg you.' It was my salvation, my only chance at being truly free. But my voice was choked with fear, and you didn't hear me, Mr X. And the next day, and the next, I dared not speak again; no, I didn't dare. And so my fate was sealed!"

The only two things I perceive with some degree of reality are her cold hair brushing against my face, and the convulsive trembling of her arms around my neck. As for the rest: that melodious, hesitant voice; the flames belched out by the chimney; the high, blackened walls; the furniture in shadows; the tears, now cold, against my flesh . . . all confused, ghastly witnesses to the pain of a contemptible woman whose suffering is inhuman, whose pain is nothing like mankind's.

"My fate was sealed! My fate was sealed!" she insists, clinging to me.

And once again, above in the darkness, beyond the great chandelier, the melancholy repetition: "My fate was sealed!"

An inconsolable creature, infinitely wretched, the victim perhaps of some secret, monstrous torment, Margaret Rose emptied her soul in mine; and I gradually, without hope, and inevitably, like a dying man in my lethargy, give way to an ecstasy, to a certain kind of spiritual inebriation—I know not whether subconsciously, or tacitly—and a physical collapse akin to agony. However, in a moment of highly intense lucidity, capable of enlightening the brain of any man, I manage to break free of the spell of that voice from beyond the grave and violently tear myself away from this woman. I throw her down on the chair. She drops at the first blow, her weak body curled like a streamer. Her black, phenomenal eyes, fixed upon me, completely devoid of expression.

I'm able to shout:

"You're dead! You're dead! Don't you dare move about anymore, because you're dead!"

And she falls silent, infinitely sorrowful, looking me right in the eye, her gaze so like that of a dog's, it makes me shudder.

"You're dead! You're dead!" I keep shouting. "Get away from me, because you're dead!"

Standing beneath that invisible ceiling all night long, I brayed the horrid, chilling truth a thousand times, I believe. And I also believe that during the entire time, her eyes didn't once blink or move, fixed, fixed upon me, phenomenal and black.

"You're dead! You're dead!"

I couldn't say, it must have been a fit of joint madness.

Soon afterwards, Margaret Rose gracefully stretched out her long, white hand towards a bishop on the chessboard and, sliding it through the remaining pieces, she murmured tenderly, in her warm, tranquil voice:

"Checkmate."

She'd beaten me once again, and once again, we'd started another game.

Again: "Checkmate."

And so on, and so on.

"Oh, Margaret Rose! You play admirably."

And the smoke from our two cigarettes blended in with the dense ambiance, rising to the ceiling, forming beautiful, undulating clouds that were lost, perfumed and content, among the sweet, nocturnal shadows. And we laughed in confidence, and in broken phrases she evoked so many forgotten reminiscences, so many: the austere Carmelite, with her thick curls, who spoke English with a certain, sobbing cadence; the languid, solitary pines of the Via Appia, so similar, on those Roman afternoons, to tall cups of sapphire overflowing with a dense, scarlet wine; the Pinzio, with its foaming fountains; Santa Maria Maggiore, San Pietro in Vincoli; the Trevi, the Forum, the gates of black lace . . . And the pieces slid across the chessboard, the breeze moaned ever so sweetly, the moon showed its face at intervals, and an almost voluptuous well-being ran through my veins.

No, I couldn't beat her.

"Admirably, admirably . . . " I finally avow, giving up once and for all.

But unexpectedly—just as dawn was breaking—Margaret Rose looked at me, terrified, pale as a lump of marble. Her eyes began to roll back in their sockets, her arms trembling convulsively. I cannot tell what manner of fiendish bird within her has begun to awaken and show itself. She gnashes her teeth, she moans, her neck muscles strain, she tries to push away the table with rigid legs, she straightens up slightly, she laughs and in the end, she lets out a ghastly, incredibly prolonged scream, that races through the chamber and flees out into the house. Fixed, fixed upon me, her phenomenal eyes seem incapable of tearing themselves away from something that has captivated them, something that subjugates them, frightens them, and irresistibly subdues them. I leap to my feet, shocked, comprehending that something very serious is going on: I call her uselessly by name, I shake her shoulders; but her arms are cold, so cold and her forehead covered with sweat.

Time goes by, and still that scream writhes among the trees outside.

"Margaret! Margaret Rose!" I implore.

Those fixed, irrational eyes.

"Margaret Rose!"

Footsteps sound close by, and a door opens. Out of the darkness, through I know not what drapes or shadows, emerges a man in pajamas: tall, young, athletic. He's barefoot and his disheveled hair falls across his forehead. Understandably distressed, he doesn't notice me. Quite the opposite; he rushes quickly towards the young woman by my side. He caresses her, he kisses her, he arranges a few loose hairs behind her ear. He sits down on the arm of her chair.

"Margaret Rose . . . My poor Margaret Rose . . . " he says to her persuasively, painfully, while ceaselessly stroking her forehead with his hand.

"Sir!" I decide to call out, my eyelids feverishly twitching.

But the man caressing that limp, perspiring body still doesn't notice me.

"Margaret Rose, go to sleep now, darling. You'll play chess some other time, all right? Margaret Rose, now do as I say."

"Sir!" I shout a second time, with all my might. "Sir!"

Margaret Rose softly opens her eyes and, seeing me stand before her, goes back to screaming as frantically as before, while pointing her finger at me.

"James! There he is, there! Just look at him!"

And she faints dead away.

Her husband looks towards where I am—nearly brushing against his back—and sadly shakes his head. Then, wife in arms, he mysteriously moves past me. And I watch them disappear, lugubriously, silently, slowly, between the red drapes.

And I realize, alarmed, that I am nothing but a melancholy, horrifying ghost.

Translated by Tanya Huntington

SCENES FROM
MEXICAN REALITY

The Mist

JUAN DE LA CABADA

For some time now, ever since I became rich during the god-damn World War and then got married, and then along came the kids, I haven't been much good anymore at telling stories. I used to tell them well. Ah, back when I was free! But now, on the other hand . . . the children! Just the thought of setting a bad example mortifies me! Why all this indecision? Perhaps it's because I've grown accustomed, in my profession, to the testimony of his lordship the priest, or the notary, or the judge, or anyone else for that matter. "There's Mr. So-and-So, let him tell it."

And yet there I was, no witnesses, racing alone down a dark highway on one of those foggy and often rainy nights.

Yes: behind the wheel of my automobile, staring at the shafts of light that spilled out from the vehicle's headlamps. I was in a hurry—barely able to contain my rage, my dark thoughts, or a certain inexplicable fear—when I realized that the dull lights from several lanterns were blocking my path. It looked as if people were holding them in their hands, swinging them across the width of the road.

No whistles, no sirens, no voices to corroborate that some unfortunate accident had occurred. "They wouldn't be trying to rob me? And who's to say that they're alone? There'll be ac-complices, hidden on either side. So therefore, therefore . . . if

I keep going and run them over, the others will shoot me in the back. Oh, what the hell! I've a loaded revolver here beside me, after all. Why suffer, then, from fear or similar afflictions? I was bound to use it sometime," I thought. I readied my weapon, and stopped the car.

"Who goes there?" I said roughly, in a loud voice.

The men with lanterns came closer.

They looked to me like four miserable Indians, the kind you recognize immediately as being prototypical construction workers: half industrialized, half men of the fields.

By the light of my reflectors, I could see eight huaraches on their feet as they approached. Their remaining apparel consisted of blue overalls, straw hats, and colored bandanas tied around their necks.

"Who goes there?" I yelled at them again.

As they drew near, raising their lanterns high, I stuck my pistol into the waistband of my trousers, so I could get the drop on them in the event of dire need. I also prepared myself by undoing the three lower buttons of my vest, just in case.

"Who goes there?" I yelled once again, as soon as they were close enough for me to see their faces.

The eldest was truly an old geezer; he wore a great, drooping moustache. Two of them looked about thirty years old, and the last, the youngest, was under twenty.

"Chief," the old man said, "we need a ride to Mexico City, 'cause we gotta show up for work real early Monday morning. That's tomorrow."

Have I not said it before? Perhaps I neglected to say from the start that this particular March evening, which found me on my way back after having gathered my strength during a weekend excursion, was a Sunday. I thought I did, didn't I?

After hearing the old man's words—scalded by the fright

they'd given me and moved by a punctilious, rather logical desire for revenge—I emitted certain mocking, disdainful noises while at the same time shaking my head in equally significant denial.

"We're running late, chief," one of the other Indians added.

It was best to take a moment and think it over, tormenting them a little in the meantime. Therefore, I neither agreed nor deigned to voice my refusal.

"Please, chief, there are no more busses coming by and since you are going in the same direction."

The youngest intervened:

"We're only builders." And he smiled innocently. Or maliciously, in veiled allusion.

I noted his mocking eyes in a face that was only too perceptive, and his insinuation became so clear to me, that refusing them would have been tantamount to showing signs of fear and debasement. Anything but that!

"You three, climb in back!" I commanded. "You, old man, ride up front with me."

Quickly, they extinguished their lanterns and rushed to obey my orders.

A light rain continued to fall.

I released the hand brake, accelerated, and continued on my way.

From behind came only four phrases. I remember them well:

"I wonder how Usebita's doing?"

"Well, you know."

"So pretty."

"Real bright, for a seven-year-old."

And from that moment on, they became entrenched in stubborn silence. Not one chuckle, not the slightest sign of openness or frankness common among those who inhabit other lands. Only a silence that leads to unrest, distrust, and suspicion; bending, straining, crushing spirits. That, and darkness skirting the edge of continuous precipices . . . those environs . . . that tenacious, funereal mist, or even the lanterns whose image burned into my retina still, their opaque lights trembling in the fog.

From a distance, the old man's breath had already given off the stench of an alcohol so cheap that now, close up, it made me feel unbearably nauseous when he turned and spoke to me —just another drunk Indian.

"This drizzle won't make it even four fingers down into the earth, right, chief?"

"Mmph!" I answered, holding my breath.

After a brief silence, he insisted:

"Not two fingers, not two fingers, wouldn't you say, chief?"

"Drunk Indian," I thought again, and didn't answer.

"Wouldn't you say, chief?"

"Yes, certainly," I said. I'd have to be patient.

Another interval, and more of the same:

"Not even this much, eh, chief?"

And then, every so often:

"Well now, not even that much, couldn't be, not even that much. No sirree."

I ran the car full throttle, afraid once again. Such is instinct! You know only too well how Indians are, with their backward speech. And by the same token, what was this one saying, or trying to say to the others, who remained motionless, fixed in their stubborn silence?

If only they were stones, harmless stones . . . but they're human beings!

Incidentally, the light rain continued, and the highway was deserted under the cold blackness of a dense fog.

I felt gusts of fear, dispelled by the secure thought of my revolver.

"Not two fingers, eh, chief?"

"Mm-hmmm!"

"Not one."

"Mmph!"

And he persisted:

"Not even one. Not one finger, not even this much."

"Sure."

"Because God sends this drizzle just to freshen the crops."

"Naturally."

"To freshen the crops, and not so much for soaking into the ground, right?"

"Right."

"Right? Isn't that right, chief?"

All of a sudden, the motor of my automobile began to show signs of overheating.

Once we'd reached the next town, I stopped and informed the men of the situation.

The old man offered to go on ahead to the next store and bring back a bucket of water.

And then, as harsh light bathed his distant figure outside the doorframe of the store, the youngest of the remaining three thrust his face close to my back and said to me from behind:

"Chief!"

I turned my head.

"That's my father, chief."

He paused, like all Indians do, in order to take a deep breath. Then another one said:

THE MIST

_____

"He's had a little too much to drink."

The youngest continued:

"You'll have to excuse us, he's going on that way because we just came back from our hometown. We went there to bury my baby sister. The honest truth is, we're builders, chief."

I hadn't asked for any explanation, but still, the third one added:

"He doesn't want her little soul getting wet down there, down below. Her little body."

The darkness, the mystery, the mist. The mist, the mystery, the darkness of the road continued.

Did I mention I used to have two children: a boy and a girl? Well, the girl fell ill.

And now, hard as my heart has been ever since she died, I go all soft sometimes, as I did there in the car. Whenever it rains, I recall their murmuring, word for word:

"I wonder how Usebita's doing?"

"Well, you know."

"So pretty."

"Real bright, for a seven-year-old."

Translated by Tanya Huntington

The Little Doe

José Revueltas

For Olivia

The mother's eyes opened wide with anguished intensity as she
inhaled the distant grassland smell that the wind had carried
precisely to that spot where it was possible to ascertain its fire,
the white hue of its flames. The old dead lizard, its head filled
with stones, was completely oblivious to the point of disap-
pearing completely, with branches and stones in its head, yet
longing for ancient eras that will never return.

Donkeys have those same eyes of terrible purity. She opened
them wide so as to encompass the entire plain, so as to stick
to the acacia and so they, humble and furious as they are, would
protect her, humbly, with their nails, with their teeth of hardened dust. From that burned and blackened space sweet sprouts
of weeds would rise over there, far off, where the wind was blowing now, weeds of an incredibly pale color, almost like water.
She opened them with all the despair she could find within her
spirit. She was moving towards that dead and sordid animal
that held in its head crags from before the flood. Towards that
cold and indifferent animal from which, perhaps, lengthy sobs
would arise, sobs of motionless pity, also from before the
flood.

"Get her. Get her, I'm telling you."

Likewise donkeys: a boundless purity, saintly and pure, a
purity filled with thoughts. They are like two lakes that can

hold so many things, entire rivers, and at the same time, men that shout. Even the landscape. Nothing is left out, just like today, not leaving out that ancient animal, coming in closer, drawing closer every minute.

Wide open until that delicate, calm panic arrives.

The lizard would think of its ancient property, of that boundless dwelling. Today, horribly old as it was.

"I'm telling you, we've got to aim for her."

The mother's eyes opened wide, as if they'd devour the world. The entire world was there, in her eyes filled with houses, and cities, and men with foam. Wives waited there for their luke-warm, dead husbands. There was a silence in the city, in the entire city, like an enormous sphere, and the mothers had no arms.

All the pain in the world.

The lizard thought of its own seniority as a living being, before it had only this apex of cliffs, when it was still able to move. There was a comforting mob, then. The first home. The first place. Death came, in turn, and out of all that, so distant and prior, counting up to one thousand, only the stones were left on top of its head, on top of its back, like a hard and motionless memory.

The mother opened her eyes as she fled, as if those eyes could reach far beyond her body. In fleeing, also, she breathed the grassland air again, an air so vast: over there, white fire, burning so that, later, weeds would grow. She opened her eyes in her thirst for salvation and for finding refuge next to the prehistoric animal. Then, those very eyes enveloped her like clean garments.

"Cut her off! Don't let her get to the hill!"

Maybe the old lizard wanted to move, but it couldn't, because it was being held by a dream that began many centuries before all things. It might have heard the noise.

Her small offspring danced for a moment around her, with graceful flexion, leaping, tied around her by a ring of air, unable to ever abandon her.

They thought she was asleep, even though her soul was with the angels in heaven by then.

Then, they too felt the same caressing blow—sharp, rough and sweet—of the gunshot.

"Yes," the hunter said to his associate, "if you kill the doe first, then you can kill the young, because they stay by her side."

The sun beat down on their heads.

Translated by Pablo Duarte

THE LITTLE DOE

The Medicine Man

FRANCISCO ROJAS GONZÁLEZ

Seated before me, Kai-Lan, lord of the Caribe Indian[1] huts of
Puná,[2] assumes a graceful, ape-like posture and offers me a
friendly smile; his stubby, restless hands fiddle with a reed. We
are under the roof of his palm leaf hut, erected in a clearing
in the jungle, a clearing that is a barren island, lost in an ocean
of vegetation that threatens to overflow in rustling, black waves.
As Kai-Lan listens, his eyes remain steady on my face; he appears
to read my expression better than he understands my words. At
times, when my meaning seems to penetrate the mind or heart
of the Indian, he laughs, he laughs loudly. But at other times,
when my narration turns serious, the Lacandón[3] becomes somber and is apparently interested in the conversation, participating in it with a few monosyllables or with some simple phrase
or other that he utters with difficulty.

Kai-Lan's three women are near us, his three *kikas*. Jacinta,

[1] *Caribe Indian*: the Caribe Indians were a war-like tribe that formerly
inhabited the north coast of South America and made their way to the Carib-
bean Islands. They practiced cannibalism and were enslaved by the Spanish.

[2] *Puná*: a part of the Mexican state of Chiapas in the Lacandón jungle,
inhabited by Tseltal and Lacandón tribes. *Puná* is also the Lacandón name
for the mahogany tree.

[3] *Lacandón*: a native Mayan living in the jungles of Chiapas. The *Lacandones*
had little contact with the outside world and worshipped their gods and
goddesses in small huts until the late 20th century.

nearly a child herself, and already the mother of an Indian baby—a little girl with round face and fat cheeks, still nursing; Jova, a reserved old woman, ugly and distant; and Nachak'in, a woman in full bloom: her profile arrogant, like a stone mask from Chichén-ltzá,[4] her eyes sensuous and coquettish, her body shapely, desirable in spite of her short stature and gestures so loose that they become licentious alongside the dullness of the other two.

Kneeling next to the *metate*, the stone for grinding corn, Jova slaps out large circles of corn dough; Jacinta, holding her daughter with her left arm, turns a pheasant, cut open from top to bottom, over the hot coals of a brazier, as it gives off an agreeable smell. Nachak'in, standing, dressed in her long, loose woolen shirt, looks boldly at her bustling companions.

"And that one," I asked Kai-Lan, pointing to Nachak'in, "why isn't she working?"

The Lacandón smiles, he is silent for a few seconds; in this way he gives the impression that he's searching for the proper words to use in his reply:

"She does not work during the day," he says finally, "at night she does. It is her turn to climb into Kai-Lan's hammock."

The beautiful *kika*, as though she understood the words that her husband has spoken to me in Spanish, lowers her eyes in response to my curious gaze, and peals back her lips in a terribly picaresque smile. From her short, robust neck hangs a necklace of alligator teeth.

Outside the hut, the jungle, the stage where the drama of the Lacandones unfolds. Opposite the house of Kai-Lan rises the temple of which he is high priest and at the same time acolyte

[4] *Chichén-Itzá*: a large Mayan archaeological site located in the Yucatán Peninsula of Mexico.

FRANCISCO ROJAS GONZÁLEZ

and parishioner. The temple is a hut, roofed with palm leaves; it has only one wall, facing west; inside, rustic looking benches, and upon them incensories or braziers made of crude clay, the deities that control the passions, that temper the natural phenomena which unleash themselves in the jungle with diabolical fury, tamers of beasts, sanctuary against serpents and other reptiles, and shelter from wicked men who live beyond the forests.

Next to the temple, the patch of corn, carefully cultivated; between the sides of the furrows dug with a hoe, vigorous plants rise from the ground more than a foot high; a blanket of thorny sticks protects the field from the incursion of wild boars and tapirs, and down below, among vines and roots, the river Jataté. The weather is warm and humid.

The voice of the jungle, with its unchanging tone and its stubborn will—like the sea—this tumult that has enervating effects on anyone who hears it for the first time, and that eventually becomes a pleasant flurry during the day and a soft lullaby at night, this voice borne from the beaks of birds, the throats of beasts, from brittle branches, from the song of the leaves of silk-cotton trees, from the foliage and the murderous strangler-fig that stretches its tentacles tightly around the corpulent trunks of the mahogany tree, of the *sapodilla*, as it climbs, to extract their last drop of sap for itself, from the intermittent whistling of the *nauyaca*-snake that lives in the bark of the *chacalté*, and from the wailing cry of the *sarahuato*, a grotesque and cynical little monkey that romps about with its incessant screeching, hanging from vines or clambering unbelievably in the highest boughs. In such a din one can scarcely hear a word of the Lacandón who is lord of the jungle and at the same time the weakest and most dispossessed of all that gives life to this world of frond and light, noise and silence.

In the hut of Kai-Lan, chief of Puná, I await the dish that his exquisite hospitality has offered to me, so that after this treat I may go on my way, through paths and quagmires into the green vastness and the marsh, toward the huts of Pancho Viejo, that silent, solitary, languid, Lacandón gentleman whose hut, bereft of *kikas*, rises down the Jataté river, a few kilometers from the lands of my present host. I figure that I'll be there by nightfall.

As I'm finishing off the breast of pheasant, Kai-Lan shows signs of uneasiness. He turns toward the jungle. He crinkles up his nose like a carnivorous animal catching the scent of something; he gets to his feet, and slowly walks outside. I watch as he questions the clouds; then, from the ground, he picks up a small stick and holds it between his thumb and first finger; through the arch formed by his fingers, the sun can be seen, nearly at its zenith.

Kai-Lan has turned around, and he tells me the result of his observation.

"You will not go far. Water is coming, much water."

I insist that I must reach the huts of Pancho Viejo that very evening, but Kai-Lan hammers on cordially.

"Look, water comes soon," and he shows me the stick through which he has observed the clouds.

"Pancho Viejo is expecting me."

Kai-Lan no longer speaks.

I have risen to my feet. I stroke the cheek of the tiny one who has fallen asleep in her mother's arms, and as I prepare to leave, enormous drops of water stop me; the storm has unleashed itself. Kai-Lan smiles as he sees his prediction carried out: "Water . . . much water."

Immediately, beneath a ceiling the color of steel that has thrust itself between the jungle and the sun, a thunderbolt roars; the storm descends upon the profusion of tree branches scraping against the crusts of clouds. The voice of the jungle becomes hushed so that the clamor of the downpour of rain may be heard. The hut shudders violently; Kai-Lan sits down again, next to me; I am caught up by the spectacle that I'm witnessing for the first time.

The water rises visibly. Jacinta has left her child lying on Kai-Lan's hammock, and followed by Jova, with innocent lewdness they lift their skirts above the waist and begin to set up a dike inside the hut to stop the water from running in. Nachak'in, the *kika* this time, passes the time squatting in a corner of the hut. Kai-Lan, with chin in his hands, watches as the storm increases in intensity and rumbling.

"What do you want at Pancho Viejo's?" he suddenly asks me.

Without much desire to draw out the conversation, I answer somewhat sharply:

"He's going to tell me things about the life of you Caribe Indians."

"And what do you care? There is no reason to meddle in the lives of neighbors!" says the Lacandón without trying to wound me.

I do not reply.

Jacinta has taken her little daughter in her arms and holds her close to her breast; now there are shadows of worry on the young woman's face. Stoically, Jova begins cutting apart an enormous *sarahuato*. The animal's pelt, pierced by one of Kai-Lan's arrows, comes falling off the reddish flesh until a naked body is left, very similar in volume and close in form to that of the chubby-cheeked little Indian girl crying in Jacinta's arms.

Kai-Lan has asked me for a cigarette and from it he puffs great clouds of smoke that, as soon as they leave his mouth, are swept away by the storm.

In the meantime the sky has never ceased spilling its water-pouch out over the jungle. The clouds become a blur with the tops of the *chacalté* and the *sapota*-tree. A bolt of lightning has split apart the trunk of a centenary silk-cotton tree like a common piece of bamboo. The crash stuns us, and for a few seconds the livid light leaves us blinded.

In the hut no one speaks. The superstitious fear of the Indians is less than my fright as a civilized man.

"Water, much water," Kai-Lan finally remarks.

Suddenly a drawn-out noise puts the finishing touch on our uneasiness. It is rotund like the sound of rocks wrenching apart. It is absolute, like the thunder of one hundred mahogany tree trunks shattering in unison.

Kai-Lan stands up, he peers outside through the thick curtain unfurled by the storm. He speaks to the women in Lacandón, and they look out to the place where the man is pointing. I do the same.

"The river, it is the river," Kai-Lan says to me in Spanish.

In fact, the Jataté has become swollen; its waters hurl along tree trunks, branches, stones as though they were straw.

The Lacandón speaks once more to his wives; they listen without a word. Jova goes to the rear of the hut and mixes together a pile of dry earth with her hands, while Kai-Lan, carrying a large gourd, walks out into the storm and immediately returns, his hair, soaking wet, dangling down past his shoulders. The shirt sticks to his body, making him appear ridiculous. Now, over the earth he pours the water from the gourd that he has brought inside. The women watch him, filled with devotion. Kai-Lan repeats the process again and again. The water and earth have become clay that the small man kneads. When he has come to the point where the clay is doughy and malleable, he sets out once again into the center of the storm. We watch him go into the temple and break apart the brazier deities with mystical fury. As soon as he has finished with the last one, he comes back to the hut.

"The gods are old . . . they are useless now," he tells me. "I will make another one, strong and brave, who will put an end to the water."

And, stretched out before the mound of clay, Kai-Lan, with unexpected mastery, begins to mold a new incensory, a magnificent and powerful god, capable of exorcising the clouds that now unleash themselves upon the huts and the river.

Discreetly, the *kikas* have turned their backs to the man. They speak to one another in hushed tones. Suddenly Nachak'in risks a glance that Kai-Lan catches sight of. The small man has risen to his feet, he shouts harshly, he claps his hands in the air, overcome with rage. Nachak'in, facing the wall again, her head down, humbly endures the reprimand. Convulsed with anger, Kai-Lan has torn apart the work that is nearly finished. God has succumbed once more to the hands of man.

After the Lacandón has made certain that the impure eye of the females will not defile the divine work, he tries to construct it once again.

And there it is, a beautiful incensory of zoomorphic appearance. A potbellied bird, its back sunken in the shape of a saucepan, the tiny figure holds itself erect on three feet that end in cleft hooves like those of a boar. Two chips of flint gleam from deep within their cavities. Kai-Lan shows that he is well satisfied with his work. He looks it up and down. He touches it again, he smooths its surface. He studies it at a distance, from every angle. And finally he conceals it under the flounce of his tunic, and goes out with it, into the storm, toward the temple. Now he is there. I see him through the dim crystal of the squall. He enthrones the resplendent god, still fresh, upon the stand. On its back he throws grains of *copal* and some live coals that he picks up with two sticks from the perpetual flame burning in the center of the room. Kai-Lan remains standing, motionless, hieratic, his arms folded, his head held high.

Meanwhile, Jova stirs the fire and it crackles, the flames slightly illuminating the hut where darkness has begun to take form. The wind continues amid the groans of trees being torn apart and the thunder of torrents. The Jataté has become arrogant, its waters are rising to an alarming height. Now they threaten to overflow. Already they are lapping at the banks that protect the cornfield. Kai-Lan has seen the danger. Beneath the roof of the temple he uneasily observes the threatening attitude of the river. He turns toward the brazier, he fills it again with resin, and he waits. But the storm does not yield. The heavy clouds sway in the summits and their shadows fall over the Caribe huts. Night rushes in. I see the silhouette of Kai-Lan as he goes to the altar. He takes the god in his hands. He destroys it and then, in a rage, hurls the fragments of clay into the pools of water that have formed in front of his hut. Useless god, unworthy god, stupid god!

But Kai-Lan has left the temple and he is going to the cornfield. It is a struggle to move through the waters. Now he gets down on all fours next to the river. He looks like a tapir wallowing in the mire. He drags over large tree trunks and branches, rocks and foliage. With all of it, he shores up the planted field. His work is agonizing and ineffectual. As I start out to help him, he returns to the hut, convinced that his efforts are useless. Then, violently, he harangues the women, and they turn their faces once again toward the wall of palm leaves. The child sleeps peacefully on the hammock, her fat, little body lying among filthy, wet rags.

Kai-Lan sets himself to the task once more.

And now, before us, we have the new god that has sprung forth from his magical hands. This one is more massive than the previous one, but less beautiful. The Lacandón raises it to the level of his eyes and contemplates it for a few seconds. He seems very proud of his creation. Behind him we hear the wailing of the child who has perhaps been awakened by the sting of an insect. When Kai-Lan turns he finds the little one staring at the incensory. The Lacandón has a look of impatience that, with the baby's laughter, soon turns to a benevolent smile. He throws the incensory, now blemished by the eyes of a female, onto the floor and begins to smash it with his bare feet. When he has finally destroyed it, he cries out. Not daring to raise her head, Jacinta picks up her daughter and carries her in her arms over to the wall. Through the sleeve of her shirt she pulls out an enormous, dark teat that the child grasps. Jacinta, like the other *kikas*, has turned her face away from Kai-Lan who does not lose faith. Now he begins again.

The Indian puts so much energy into his work that he forgets about me, and I freely watch the steps in the manufacture of the god as they take place. Kai-Lan's small hands take pieces of clay, they nervously roll around balls, they mold cylinders or smooth out flat shapes; they dance over the incipient form, intent, agile, lively. Jova and Jacinta, the latter rocking the child in her arms, remain standing, their backs to us. Nachak'in, melancholy perhaps because of the frustration of her seduction, is sitting, cross-legged, facing the wall. Her head slumps, she is fast asleep. In the center of the hut the fire crackles. It is nighttime.

This time the making of the god has been more laborious. One could say that, confronted by the failures, the maker puts all his art, all his mastery to the task. He sculpts a fabulous quadruped: snout of a *nauyaca*-snake, body of a tapir and the enormous, graceful tail of a *quetzal*-bird. Now, silently, he looks at the fruit of his efforts. There it is, a magnificent beast, strong, dark, brutal. The Lacandón has risen to his feet; the incensory rests on the floor. Kai-Lan takes a few steps backward to look at it from a distance. He has noticed some imperfection that he hastens to correct with his fingers moistened with saliva. Finally, he is completely satisfied. He lifts the incensory in his arms, and when he is certain that it has not been profaned by the look of females, he smiles and prepares to take it to his altars. He brushes against my legs as he goes past; I am certain that at this instant he does not notice my presence at all.

The shadows of the rain-soaked night do not allow me to see the handiwork of Kai-Lan in his function as high priest. My eyes can barely make out the tiny, intermittent light that burns on the back of the newly-sculpted deity, and the anguished flickering of the fire, fed perpetually with wet wood.

In the meantime, Jova has built a marvelous structure of sticks next to the hearth. From it the *sarahuato* hangs, to be cooked over the embers. The appearance of the quadruped is awful. Its head, slumped over its chest seems to be grimacing; its twisted limbs remind me of figures of martyrs, of male martyrs being subjected to torture because of their saintliness or . . . their heresy. The grains of salt that spatter the flesh burst with a small, enervating crackle, while fat drips down to leave the little, anthropomorphic body black and dried out.

Jacinta, kneeling before a potbellied piece of earthenware, takes out the corn and places it on the grinding stone. The child is sleeping on a mat spread out within the mother's reach.

Nachak'in, who is seeing her night of love pass by fruitlessly, has thrown herself upon the hammock where she frets anxiously. Her legs, shapely and small, hang down and swing back and forth restlessly.

Suddenly we hear shouts coming from the cornfield. It is Kai-Lan. Jacinta and Jova respond immediately to the call; the two *kikas* go out into the storm, to where their husband is summoning them. Nachak'in barely sits up to watch them go. She yawns, she folds her arms over the head of the hammock and stretches her body like a small beast in heat.

I look out toward the field. Kai-Lan under a lush silk-cotton tree holds up a stick of candlewood whose flame, surprisingly, challenges the violent wind. The women struggle in the midst of the mud in furious battle against the water that has already risen above the small ledge that had held it back. Now the first stalks of corn are under water. I run to help the women. Immediately I find myself sunk to the waist in mud and engaged in the Lacandones' fight. While Jacinta and I bring up stones and mud, Jova builds a barrier that, more swiftly than it can be raised, is torn away by the current. Kai-Lan cries out stinging words in Lacandón; they redouble their efforts. The man comes and goes under the enormous umbrella of the silk-cotton trees; the torch, held aloft, sends out its weak light to us. A moment arrives when Kai-Lan's agitation is irrepressible. He leaves the stick of candlewood propped up between two stones and goes toward the temple-hut. He enters and leaves us engaged in our useless efforts. Jacinta has slipped and fallen. The water drags her a distance. Jova is able to grab her by the hair and with my help we pull her out of danger. An enormous tree trunk floating in the water completely sweeps away our work. The flood overflows now into rivulets that make pools of water at the feet of the maize plants. Nothing can be done. And yet, the women keep up their earnest fight. When I am at the point of leaving, absolutely exhausted, I notice that the storm is over.

It has gone just as it came, without spectacular circumstances, suddenly, just the way everything in the jungle appears or leaves: the predators, lightning, the wind, vegetation, death.

Kai-Lan emerges from the temple, he cries out jubilantly. Nachak'in peers out from the hut and celebrates her husband's happiness with laughter. We go back to the hut.

Nachak'in sees how the monkey's body is becoming scorched, is turning to char, and does nothing to stop it. A black, fetid cloud makes the air unbreathable. The child sobs, exhausted from its wailing.

The women laugh when they see how ridiculous I look: we are smeared with mud from head to foot.

I try to clean the mud from my boots. Kai-Lan offers me a gourd full of *balché*, the fermented drink that is a ritual for great occasions. I take one drink, then another and another . . . When I bend my elbow for the third time I notice that dawn is breaking.

Kai-Lan is at my side, he is looking at me amiably. Nachak'in comes up and tries to wrap her arm around the small man's neck, lewdly and provocatively. He pushes her back delicately and at the same time says to me:

"Not now Nachak'in, because today is tomorrow."

Then, softly, he calls to Jova. The old woman comes to the man submissively. He puts his arm around her waist and leaves it there. "Today Jova will not work. She will at night, because it is her turn to climb into Kai-Lan's hammock."

Then he says a few brief words to Nachak'in who has distanced herself slightly from the group. The beautiful, imperious woman, now docile and humble, goes to the hearth to take the place that Jova, whose turn it is to be *kika*, has left.

I make ready to go. I give some red combs and a mirror to the women. They show their gratitude with wide, white smiles.

Kai-Lan presents me with a thigh of monkey that escaped the scorching. I repay him with a handful of cigarettes.

I start out in the direction of the huts of the gentleman, Pancho Viejo. Kai-Lan accompanies me to the rough ground. When we pass by the temple, the Lacandón stops and, pointing to the altar, he remarks:

"There is no one, in all the jungle, like Kai-Lan for making gods. It turned out well, did it not? It killed the storm. Look, in the struggle it lost its beautiful tail of the *quetzal*-bird and left it in the sky."

In fact, caught on the bough of a tree, a rainbow appears, resplendent.

Translated by Robert S. Rudder and Gloria Arjona

THE MEDICINE MAN

Blame the Tlaxcaltecs

Nacha listened, motionless; someone was knocking at the back door. When again they persisted, she opened the door cautiously and looked out into the night. Señora Laura appeared, shushing her with a finger on her lips. She was still wearing the white dress, singed and caked with dirt and blood.

"Señora!" Nacha murmured.

Señora Laura tiptoed in and looked at the cook, her eyes puzzled. Then, feeling more assured, she sat next to the stove and looked at her kitchen as if she'd never seen it before.

"Nachita, give me some coffee. I'm freezing."

"Missus, your husband . . . your husband is going to kill you. We'd already given you up for dead."

"For dead?"

Laura looked at the white tiles of the kitchen with amazement, put her legs up on the chair, hugged her knees. She grew thoughtful. Nacha put water on and watched her mistress out of the corner of her eye; she couldn't think of a single thing to say. The señora rested her head on her knees; she seemed so sad.

"You know, Nacha, you can blame the Tlaxcaltecs."[1]

---

[1] *Tlaxcaltecs*: an indigenous group from Tlaxcala in Mexico, who aided the 16th century Spanish conquistadors, led by Hernán Cortés.

Nacha didn't answer; she chose to watch the pot, which hadn't boiled.

Outside, night had blurred the roses in the garden and cast shadows across the fig trees. The lighted windows of neighboring houses shone far beyond the branches. The kitchen was kept separate from the world by an invisible wall of sadness, by no more than a bar rest.

"Don't you agree, Nacha?"

"Yes, ma'am."

"I'm no different from them. I'm a traitor," Laura said, mournfully.

The cook folded her arms, waiting for the water to start bubbling.

"And you, Nacha, are you a traitor?"

She looked at her, hopefully. If Nacha shared with her this capacity for betrayal, then Nacha would understand her, and tonight Laura needed someone to understand her.

Nacha thought about it for a moment and went back to watching the water that now boiled noisily. She poured it over the coffee and its warm smell made her feel attuned to her mistress.

"Yes, I'm a traitor too, Señora Laurita."

She poured the coffee, happily, into a little cup, put in two cubes of sugar and set it in front of the señora. And she, in turn lost in her own thoughts, took a few sips.

"You know, Nachita, now I know why we had so many accidents on our famous trip to Guanajuato. At Mil Cumbres we ran out of gas. Margarita got frightened because it was getting dark. A truck driver gave us some gas to get us to Morelia. In Cuitzeo, when we were crossing the white bridge, the car stopped suddenly. Margarita was annoyed with me. You know how lonely roads and the eyes of Indians frighten her. When a car full of tourists came by, she went into town to look for a mechanic and I was stuck in the middle of the white bridge that crosses the dry lake and its bed of flat white rocks. The light was very white and the bridge, the rocks and the car began to float in it. Then the light broke into pieces until it became thousands of small dots and began to whirl until it was fixed in place like a picture. Time had entirely turned around, like it does when you see a postcard and then turn it to see what's written on the other side. That's how, at Cuitzeo Lake, I got to the child I'd been. The light brings about crises like that, when the sun turns white and you are in the very center of its rays. Thoughts, too, become thousands of small dots, and you get dizzy. At that moment I looked at the fabric of my white dress and, just then, heard his steps. I wasn't surprised. I looked up and saw him coming. In that same instant I remembered how serious my treachery had been; I was frightened and wanted to escape. But time closed in around me, it became singular and transitory, and I couldn't move from the seat of my car. When I was a child I was told, 'Some day you will find yourself faced with your acts turned to stones that are as irrevocable as that one,' and they showed me the statue of some god, though I can't remember now which one it was. We forget everything, don't we, Nachita, although we only forget for a time. In those days, even words seemed to be of stone, although of a stone that was liquid and clear. The stone hardened as each word was pronounced, and it was written for always in time. Weren't the words of your grown-ups like that?"

Nacha thought about it for a moment, then agreed, fully convinced.

"They were, Señora Laurita."

"The terrible thing is—and I discovered it that very moment—that everything that is unbelievable is true. He was coming, along the side of the bridge, sunburned and carrying the weight of defeat on his naked shoulders. His eyes shone. Their black sparks reached me from the distance and his black hair curled in the white light of our meeting. Before I could do anything about it, he was in front of me. He stopped, held on to the car door and looked at me. He had a cut in his left hand and the blood that spurted from the wound in his shoulder was so red it seemed black. He didn't say anything to me. But I knew he was escaping, and that he had been beaten. He wanted to tell me I deserved to die, and at the same time, that my death would bring about his own. As wounded as he was, he was looking for me.

" 'You can blame the Tlaxcaltecs,' I told him.

"He turned to look up at the sky. Then he focused his eyes on mine again.

" 'What are you doing to yourself,' he asked, in a deep voice. I couldn't tell him I'd married, because I am married to him. There are things that just can't be said, you know that, Nachita.

" 'And the others?' I asked him.

" 'The ones who got out alive are in the same shape I am.' I saw that each word pained his mouth and I hushed, realizing the shamefulness of my treachery.

" 'You know I'm frightened and that's why I betray you.'

" 'I know,' he answered, and bowed his head. He's known me since I was a girl, Nacha. His father and mine were brothers and so we are cousins. He always loved me, at least that's what he said and that's what we all believed. At the bridge, I was embarrassed. The blood kept on flowing down his chest. I took a small handkerchief from my bag and, without saying a word, began to wipe the blood. I always loved him too, Nachita, because he is the very opposite of me. He's not fearful and he's not a traitor. He took my hand and looked at it.

" 'It's very pale; it looks like their hands,' he told me.

" 'I haven't gotten any sun for a while.' He lowered his eyes and let my hand drop. We stayed like that, in silence, listening to the blood flowing down his chest, he didn't reproach me for anything; he knows what I'm capable of. But the little threads of blood wrote a message on his chest, that his heart had preserved my words and my body. That's when I knew, Nachita, that time and love are the same thing.

" 'And my house?' I asked.

" 'We'll go see it.' He held me with his hot hand the way he would hold his shield, and I realized he wasn't carrying it. 'He lost it when he was escaping,' I told myself, and I let him guide me. In the light of Cuitzeo, his footsteps sounded the way they had in the other light: muffled and soft. We walked through the city that blazed on the water's edge. I closed my eyes. I already told you I'm a coward, Nacha. Or perhaps it was the smoke and the dust that made my eyes water. I sat on a stone and covered my face with my hands.

" 'I can't walk any more,' I told him.

" 'We're almost there,' he answered. He knelt by me and caressed my white dress with his fingertips.

" 'If you don't want to see what happened, don't look,' he told me, quietly.

"His black hair shadowed me. He wasn't angry, only sad. I would never have dared to embrace him before, but now I've learned I don't have to be respectful of the man, so I embraced his neck and kissed him on the mouth.

" 'You've always been dearest of all things to my heart,' he said. He lowered his head and looked at the earth, so full of dry stones. With one of them he drew two parallel lines and then lengthened them until they met and became one.

" 'These are you and me,' he said without looking up. I was left at a loss for words, Nachita.

" 'There's only a little left for time to be over and for us to be one. That's why I was looking for you.' I had forgotten, Nacha, that when time is all spent, the two of us will remain, one in the other, to enter true time as one. When he said that to me, I looked in his eyes. Before I had only dared to look in them when he was taking me, but, as I told you, I've learned not to respect the man's eyes. It's also true that I didn't want to see what was happening around me. I'm such a coward. I remembered the shrieks and I heard them again, strident, flaming in the middle of the morning. I also saw the stones whiz over my head and heard them crashing. He knelt in front of me and raised his arms and crossed them to make a little roof over my head.

" 'This is the end of man,' I said.

" 'That's true,' he said, with his voice over mine. And I saw myself in his eyes and in his body. Could he be a deer come to carry me to its hillside? Or a star, flinging me out to trace signs in the sky? His voice traced signs of blood on my breast, and my white dress turned tiger-striped in red and white.

" 'I'll return tonight; wait for me,' he whispered. He grasped his shield and looked at me from high above.

" 'Soon we'll be one,' he added, with his usual politeness. After he left, I began to hear battle cries again and I ran out in the middle of the rain of stones and was lost all the way to the car, parked on the Cuitzeo Lake Bridge.

" 'What's the matter? Are you wounded?' Margarita shouted at me when she arrived. Frightened, she touched the blood on my white dress and pointed to the blood on my lips and the dirt that matted my hair. The dead eyes of the Cuitzeo mechanic stared at me from the other car.

" 'Indian savages! A woman can't be left alone,' he muttered as he leapt from the car as if to help me.

"We arrived at Mexico City at nightfall. How it had changed,

Nachita, I couldn't believe it! At noon the warriors had been there, but now there wasn't even a trace of them. There was no rubble left either. We passed the sad and silent Zócalo; nothing —nothing!—remained of the other plaza. Margarita watched me out of the corner of her eye. When we got home you opened the door. Remember?"

Nacha nodded her head, agreeing. It was quite true that, barely two months before, Señora Laurita and her mother-in-law had gone to Guanajuato on a visit. The night they returned, they, Josefina the chamber maid and she herself, had noticed the blood on the dress and the señora's vacant gaze. Margarita, the older lady, motioned them to keep quiet. She seemed very worried. Josefina told her later that, at dinner, the master stared at his wife in annoyance and said, "Why don't you change your clothes? Do you enjoy returning to unpleasant memories?"

Señora Margarita, his mother, had already told him what happened and motioned to him, as if to say "Hush, have a little consideration." Señora Laurita didn't answer; she stroked her lips and smiled as if she knew something. Then the master went back to talking about president López Mateos.

"You know how he's always talking about that man," Josefina had added, contemptuously.

In their hearts, they were sure that Señora Laurita was bored with so much talk about the president and his official visits.

"How odd things are, Nachita, I'd never noticed until that night how bored I could be with Pablo," the mistress noted, hugging her knees affectionately, and subtly acknowledging that Josefina and Nachita were right.

The cook folded her arms and nodded in agreement.

"From the time I entered the house, the furniture, the vases and the mirror toppled over on me and left me sadder than I was. How many days, how many years will I have to wait before my cousin comes to fetch me? That's what I told myself, and I regretted my treachery. As we dined, I noticed that Pablo did not speak in words but in letters. I started to count them while I watched his thick mouth and dead eye. Suddenly, he was silent. You know he forgets everything. He stood there with his arms by his side. 'This new husband has no memory and all he knows are the day in, day out things.'

" 'You have a troubled and confused husband,' he told me, looking at the stains on my dress again. My poor mother-in-law got embarassed and, as we were drinking coffee, she got up to play a twist.

" 'To cheer you up,' she told us, pretending to smile because she could tell trouble was brewing.

"We didn't talk. The house filled up with noise. I looked at Pablo. 'He looks like . . . ' and I didn't dare to say his name because I was afraid that they would read my mind. It's true that they look alike, Nacha. Both of them like rain and cool houses. The two of them look at the sky in the afternoon and have black hair and white teeth. But Pablo talks in fits and starts, he gets angry about anything, and is always asking, 'What are you thinking?' My cousin husband doesn't do or say anything like that."

"That's for sure. It's true that the boss is a pain in the neck," Nacha said with annoyance.

Laura sighed and looked with a sense of relief at her cook. At least she could confide in her.

"At night, while Pablo kissed me, I kept repeating to myself, 'When will he come for me?' And I almost cried, recalling the blood streaming from the wound in his shoulder. Neither could I forget his arms folded over my head that made a little roof for me. At the same time I was afraid that Pablo would notice that my cousin had kissed me that morning. But he didn't notice a thing, and if it hadn't been that Josefina had frightened me in the morning, Pablo would never have known."

Nachita agreed. That Josefina loved to start trouble; she was to blame. Nacha had told her, "Be quiet, be quiet, for God's sake. There must have been a reason they didn't hear us scream." But it was useless.

No sooner had Josefina come into the bosses' room with the breakfast tray than she told what she should have kept to herself.

"Missus, last night a man was peeking through your bedroom window. Nacha and I screamed and screamed!"

"We didn't hear anything," the master said. He was shocked.

"It was he," that fool of a mistress screeched.

"Who is he?" the master asked, looking at the señora as if he wanted to kill her. At least that's what Josefina said later.

The señora was really scared. She covered her mouth with her hand, and when the boss asked her the same question again —he was getting angrier and angrier—she answered, "The Indian, the Indian who followed me from Cuitzeo to Mexico City."

That's how Josefina found out the business about the Indian and that's how she told Nachita.

"We have to let the police know immediately!" the boss yelled.

Josefina showed them the window the stranger had been looking through and Pablo examined it closely. There were almost-fresh blood stains on the window sill.

"He's wounded," señor Pablo said in a worried tone. He took a few steps around the bedroom and stopped in front of his wife.

"It was an Indian, sir," Josefina said, just as Laura had said. Pablo saw the white dress thrown over a chair and picked it up roughly.

"Can you tell me where these stains came from?"

The señora was silent, looking at the blood stains on the bodice of the dress while the master punched the chest of drawers with his fist. Then he went to his wife and slapped her. Josefina saw and heard all that.

"He's rough and his actions are as confused as his thoughts. It's not my fault he accepted defeat," Laura said disdainfully.

"That's true," Nachita agreed.

There was a long silence in the kitchen. Laura stuck the tip of her finger in the bottom of the cup to stir the black grounds that had settled, and when Nacha saw this, she poured her a nice fresh cup of hot coffee.

"Drink your coffee, Señora," she said, feeling sorry for her mistress's unhappiness. After all, what was the boss complaining about? You could see from miles away that Señora Laurita wasn't meant for him.

"I fell in love with Pablo on a road, during a moment when he reminded me of someone I knew, someone I couldn't remember. And later, just sometimes, I recaptured the moment when it seemed that he would become the one he resembled. But it wasn't true. He became absurd again, without a memory, and he only repeated the gestures of all the men of Mexico City. How did you expect me not to notice the deception? When he's angry, he doesn't allow me to leave the house. You know it's true. How many times has he started arguments at the movies or at restaurants! You know, Nachita. On the other hand, my cousin husband never gets angry at his wife."

Nacha knew what the señora was saying was true, and that was why that morning when Josefina had come in the kitchen, scared and screaming, "Wake up Señora Margarita, the master is beating the mistress," Nacha, had run to the older woman's bedroom.

His mother's presence calmed Señor Pablo. Margarita was very surprised to hear the business about the Indian, since she hadn't seen him at Cuitzeo Lake and had only seen the blood, as we all had.

"Perhaps you suffered from sunstroke at the lake, Laura, and had a nosebleed. We had the top down on the car, you know, son." She talked almost without knowing what to say.

Señora Laura flung herself face down on the bed and was lost in her own thoughts while her husband and her mother-in-law argued.

"Do you know what I was thinking this morning, Nachita? Suppose he saw me last night when Pablo was kissing me. And I felt like crying. Just then I remembered that when a man and a woman love each other and they have no children, they are condemned to become one. That's what my other father told me when I brought him a drink of water and he looked at the door behind which my cousin husband and I slept. Everything my other father had told me was coming true. I could hear Pablo and Margarita's words from my pillow and they were talking foolishness. 'I'm going to fetch him,' I told myself. 'But, where?' Later, when you returned to my room to ask me what we were going to do about dinner, a thought came to my head, 'Go to the Tacuba Café.' And I didn't even know that café, Nachita, I'd only heard it mentioned."

Nacha remembered the señora as if she could see her now, putting on her white, blood-stained dress, the same one she was wearing in the kitchen now.

"For God's sakes, Laura, don't put that dress on," her mother-in-law said. But she didn't pay any attention. To hide the stains, she put a white sweater on over it, buttoned up to the neck, and left for the street without saying goodbye. The worst came later. No, not the worst. The worst was about to happen now in the kitchen, if Señora Margarita happened to wake up.

"There was no one in the Tacuba Café. That place is dismal, Nachita. A waiter came up to me.

" 'What would you like?' I didn't want anything but I had to ask for something.

" 'Some coconut nougat.'

"My cousin and I used to eat coconut when we were small. A clock in the café told time. 'In all the cities, there are clocks telling time; it must be wearing away bit by bit. When it only exists as a transparent layer, he will arrive and the two lines he traced will become one and I will live in the dearest chamber of his heart.' That's what I told myself as I ate the nougat.

" 'What time is it?,' I asked the waiter.

" 'Twelve, Miss.'

" 'Pablo arrives at one,' I told myself. 'If I have a taxi take me outside of town, I can wait a little longer.' But I didn't wait and I went out on the street. The sun was silver. My thoughts turned into shining dust and there was no present, past, nor future. My cousin was on the sidewalk. He stood in front of me. He looked at me for a long time with his sad eyes.

" 'What are you doing?' he asked me in his deep voice.

" 'I was waiting for you.'

"He was as still as a panther. I saw his black hair and the wound on his shoulder.

" 'Weren't you afraid to be here all by yourself?'

"The stones and the shouts buzzed around us again and I felt something burn against my back. 'Don't look,' he told me.

"He knelt on the ground and put out the flame that had started to blaze on my dress. I saw the despair in his eyes.

" 'Get me out of here!' I screamed with all my might, because I remembered I was in front of my father's house, that the house was burning and that my parents were in the back and my little brothers were dead. I could see everything reflected in his eyes while he knelt in the dirt putting out the fire on my dress. I allowed myself to fall on him and he gathered me in his arms. He covered my eyes with his hot hand.

" 'This is the end of man,' I told him, my eyes still under his hand.

" 'Don't look at it!'

"He held me against his heart. I could hear it pound like thunder rolling in the mountains. How long would it be before time was over and I would hear him forever. My tears cooled his hand, still burning from the fire in the city. The shrieks and the stones surrounded us, but I was safe against his breast.

" 'Sleep with me,' he said in a very low voice.

" 'Did you see me last night?' I asked him.

" 'I saw you.'

"We fell asleep in the morning light, in the heat of the fire. When we remembered, he got up and grabbed his shield.

" 'Hide until morning. I'll come for you.'

"He ran off quickly, his legs still naked. And I slipped away again, Nachita, because I was frightened when I was alone.

" 'Are you feeling bad, Miss?'

"A voice just like Pablo's approached me on the middle of the street.

" 'How dare you? Leave me alone.'

"I took a taxi that drove by the outskirts to bring me home and I got here."

Nacha remembered her arrival. She had opened the door herself, and it was she who gave her the news. Josefina came down later, almost diving down the stairs.

"Missus, the master and Señora Margarita are at the police station."

Laura stared at her, wordless in amazement.

"Where were you, Missus?"

"I went to the Tacuba Café."

"But that was two days ago."

Josefina had *Today's News* with her. She read in a loud voice, "Mrs. Aldama's whereabouts remain unknown. It is believed that the sinister, Indian-looking man who followed her from Cuitzeo may be a psychopath. The police in the states of Michoacán and Guanajuato are investigating the event."

Señora Laurita grabbed the newspaper from Josefina's hands and tore it angrily. Then she went to her room. Nacha and Josefina followed her; it was best not to leave her alone. They saw her throw herself on the bed and start dreaming with her eyes wide open. The two had the very same thought and told each other so in the kitchen. "As far as I'm concerned, Señora Laurita is in love." When the master arrived they were still in their mistress's room.

"Laura!" he shouted. He rushed to the bed and took his wife in his arms.

"Heart of my heart," the man sobbed.

For a moment, Señora Laurita seemed to soften towards him.

"Señor," Josefina blustered. "The Señora's dress is completely scorched!"

Nacha looked at her, disapprovingly. The master checked over the señora's dress and legs.

"It's true. Even the soles of her shoes are singed. What happened, my love, where were you?"

"At the Tacuba Café," the señora answered calmly.

Señora Margarita twisted her hands and approached her daughter-in-law.

"We know you were there and that you had some nougat. What happened then?"

"I took a taxi and drove home past the outskirts of town."

Nacha lowered her eyes. Josefina opened her mouth as if to say something, and Señora Margarita bit her lip. Pablo reacted differently; he grabbed his wife by her shoulders and shook her violently.

"Stop acting like an idiot! Where were you for two days? Why is your dress burned?"

"Burned? But he extinguished it . . . " The words slipped out of Señora Laura's mouth.

"He? That filthy Indian?" Pablo went back to shaking her in anger.

"I met him at the door to the Tacuba Café," the señora sobbed, half dead of fear.

"I didn't think you'd stoop so low," the boss said and pushed her onto the bed.

"Tell us who he is," her mother-in-law said, softening her voice.

"I couldn't tell them that he was my husband, could I, Nacha?" Laura asked, wanting the cook's approval.

Nacha approved of the señora's discretion and remembered how, at noontime, and, saddened by what her mistress' was going through, she had said, "Perhaps the Cuitzeo Indian is a witch man."

But Señora Margarita had turned towards her with her eyes blazing, to scream an answer, "A witch man! You mean a murderer!"

After that, they kept Señora Laurita in the house for days. The master ordered them to watch the doors and windows. They, the maids, went in and out of the room continuously to check on her. Nacha never discussed the situation or the odd, surprising things she'd seen. But who could silence Josefina?

"Master, this morning at dawn the Indian was by the window again," she announced when she took in the breakfast tray.

The master rushed to the window and again found a trace of fresh blood. The señora began to cry.

"My poor little one, my poor little one," she sobbed.

It was that afternoon that the master brought a doctor. After that, the doctor came every afternoon.

"He asked me about my childhood, about my father and mother. But, Nachita, I didn't know which childhood he meant, or which father or mother he wanted to know about. That's why I talked to him about the conquest of Mexico. You understand me, don't you?" Laura asked, keeping her eyes on the yellow bowls.

"Yes, ma'am," and Nachita, feeling nervous, examined the garden through the window glass. Night was just beginning to announce its presence in the deepening shadows. She remembered the master's listless face and his mother's distressed glances at dinner.

"Laura asked the doctor for Bernal Díaz del Castillo's *History*. She said that that's the only thing that interests her."

Señora Margarita dropped her fork. "My poor son, your wife is mad."

"The only thing she talks about is the fall of the great Tenochtitlán,"[2] Señor Pablo added somberly.

Two days later, the doctor, Señora Margarita, and Señor Pablo decided that locking Laura in made her depression worse. She should have some contact with the world and face her responsibilities. From then on, the boss sent the car so his wife could take short rides around Chapultepec Park.

[2] *The great Tenochtitlán*: capital of the Aztec empire, whose ruins lie within modern-day Mexico City.

The señora was accompanied by her mother-in-law, and the chauffeur had orders to watch them closely. Unfortunately the eucalyptus-laden atmosphere didn't improve her condition, and no sooner would Señora Laurita get back home than she would lock herself up in her room to read Bernal Díaz's *Conquest of Mexico*.

One morning, Señora Margarita came back from Chapultepec Park alone and frantic. "That crazy woman ran away," she shouted in a huge voice.

"Look, Nacha, I sat on the same bench as usual and told myself, 'He won't forgive me. A man can forgive one, two, three, four betrayals but not constant betrayal.' This made me very sad. It was very hot and Margarita bought herself some vanilla ice cream. I didn't want any and she got into the car to eat it. I realized that she was as bored of me as I was of her. I don't like being watched and I tried to look at other things so I wouldn't see her eating her cone and watching me. I noticed the grayish foliage that hung from the *ahuehuete* trees and, I don't know why, but the morning became as sad as those trees. 'They and I have seen the same crises,' I told myself. During the lonely hours, alone on an empty path. My husband had watched my constant betrayal through the window and had abandoned me to this path made of non-existent things. I remembered the smell of corn leaves and the hushed murmur of his steps. 'This is the way he walked, with the rhythm of dry leaves when the February wind carries them over the stones. At that time I didn't have to turn my head to know that he was watching me from behind . . . ' I was meandering through those sad thoughts when I heard the sun spill and the dry leaves begin to shift. His breathing came close behind me, then he stood in front of me. I saw his naked feet in front of mine. He had a scratch on his knee. I lifted my eyes and found myself under his. We stood there a long time without speaking. Out of respect, I waited for his word.

" 'What are you doing to yourself?' he asked me.

"I saw that he wasn't moving and that he seemed sadder than ever. 'I was waiting for you,' I answered.

" 'The last day is almost here.'

"I thought that his voice came from the depth of time. Blood still surged from his shoulder. I was embarrassed and lowered my eyes. I opened my bag, and took out a small handkerchief to wipe his chest. Then I put it away again. He followed, watching me quietly.

" 'Let us go to the Tacuba door. There are many betrayals.'

"He grasped my hand and we walked among the people, who screamed and moaned. Many bodies floated in the water of the canals. Pestilence rose up around us and children cried, running from here to there, lost and looking for their parents. I looked at everything without wanting to see it. The shattered canoes didn't carry anything but sadness. The husband sat me under a broken tree. He knelt on the earth and watched what happened around us. He wasn't afraid. Then he looked at me.

" 'I know you're a traitor and that you mean well. The good grows alongside the bad.'

"The children were screaming so loudly I could hardly hear him. The sound came from far off, but it was so loud that it shattered the daylight. It seemed like the last time they would cry.

" 'It's the children,' he told me. 'This is the end of man,' I repeated, because I couldn't think of anything else to say.

"He put his hands over my ears and then held me against his chest. 'You were a traitor when I met you, and I loved you that way.'

" 'You were born without luck,' I told him. I embraced him. My cousin and husband closed his eyes to keep the tears from flowing. We lay ourselves on the broken branches of the *pirú*. The shouts of the warriors, the stones, and the weeping of the children reached us even there.

" 'Time is almost over,' my husband sighed.

"The women who didn't want to die that day were escaping through a crevice. Rows of men fell one after the other, as if clasping hands as a single blow felled them all at once. Some of them let out such loud cries that the sound echoed long after their death.

"It wasn't long before we became one that my cousin got up, joined some branches together and made me a little cave.

" 'Wait for me here.'

"He looked at me and went back to the fray, hoping to turn aside defeat. I stayed there, curled up. I didn't want to see the people escaping, so I wouldn't be tempted, and I didn't want to see the bodies floating in the water, so I wouldn't cry. I began to count the little fruits that hung from the cut branches; they were dry and when I touched them with my fingers, the red husks fell from them. I don't know why I thought they were bad luck and decided to watch the sky as it began to darken. First it turned grey, then it began to take on the color of the drowned bodies in the canal. I recalled the colors of other afternoons. But the evening grew more and more bruised, swelling as if it would soon burst, and I understood that time was over. What would happen to me if my cousin didn't return? He might have died in battle. I didn't care what happened to him, I ran out of there as fast as I could, with fright on my heels. 'When he comes back to look for me . . . ' I didn't have time to finish my thought because I found myself in the Mexico City dusk. 'Margarita must have finished her ice cream and Pablo is probably angry.' A taxi drove along the outskirts to bring me home. And you know, Nachita, the outskirts were the canals, clogged with bodies. That's why I was so sad when I got home. Now, Nachita, don't tell the master that I spent the afternoon with my husband."

Nachita arranged her arms on her purple skirt.

"Señor Pablo went to Acapulco ten days ago. He got very thin during all the weeks of the investigation," Nacha explained, feeling self-satisfied.

Laura looked at her without any surprise and sighed with relief.

"But Señora Margarita is upstairs," Nacha added, turning her eyes up to the kitchen ceiling.

Laura hugged her knees and looked through the window glass at the roses, blurred by the night shadows, and at the lights in the neighboring windows that had begun to go out.

Nacha sprinkled salt on the back of her hand and licked it eagerly.

"So many coyotes! The whole pack is in an uproar," she said, her voice full of salt.

Laura listened for a moment. "Damn animals! You should have seen them this afternoon," she said.

"As long as they don't get in the señor's path or make him lose his way," Nacha said, fearfully.

"Why should he be afraid of them tonight, he was never afraid of them before?" Laura said in annoyance.

Nacha drew closer to strengthen the intimacy that had suddenly sprung up between them. "They're punier than the Tlaxcaltecs," she told her in a soft voice.

The two women were silent. Nacha, licking bit by bit the salt on her hand, and Laura, who was worried, were both listening to the coyote howls that filled the night. It was Nacha who saw him arrive and opened the window to him.

"Señora, he's come for you," she whispered in a voice so low only Laura could hear.

Afterwards, when Laura had left with him for good, Nacha wiped the blood from the window and frightened away the coyotes, who had entered the century that was just then waning. Straining her ancient eyes, Nacha checked to see that everything was in order. She washed the coffee cup, threw the red lipstick-stained butts away in the garbage can, put the coffee pot away in the cupboard and shut off the light.

"I say Señora Laurita didn't belong to this time, and not to the master either," she said that morning when she took breakfast to Señora Margarita.

"I won't work at the Aldama house any more. I'm looking for something else," she told Josefina. And, because of the chambermaid's carelessness, Nacha left without even collecting her salary.

Translated by Ina Cumpiano

THE TANGIBLE PAST

The Dinner

The supper, that delights and enchants.
St. John of the Cross

I had to run through unknown streets. My journey's end seemed to roll just ahead of my steps, and the appointed hour was already throbbing on the public clocks. The streets were desolate. Snakes of spotlight beams danced before my eyes. At every moment circular brick flower beds sprang up, and in the artificial light of night their greenness took on a surreal elegance. I think I had seen a multitude of towers—I don't know whether in the houses or in the flower beds—displaying to the four winds, four round spheres of clock faces illuminated from within.

I was running, spurred on by a superstitious feeling about the hour. If the clocks strike nine, I said to myself, before my hand is on the door knocker, something awful will happen. And as I ran frantically I remembered having run through that place at the same hour and with a similar yearning. When?

Finally the pleasure of that false memory so absorbed me that I resumed my normal pace without realizing it. From time to time, from pauses in my musings, I saw I was in another place, and new views unfolded before me: glowing spotlights, little plazas with flowers, illuminated clock faces . . . I don't know how much time elapsed while I slept in the dizziness of my anxious breathing.

Suddenly, nine resounding peals trickled over my skin with

metallic chill. As a last hope my eyes fell upon the closest door: that was my destination.

Then to put myself in the right frame of mind, I went back over the reasons for my being there. In the morning the mail had brought me a brief and suggestive invitation. A street address was handwritten in the corner of the piece of paper. The date was yesterday's. The letter merely said:

"Doña Magdalena and her daughter Amalia await your presence to dine, tomorrow at nine p.m. Ah, if you could come!"

Not one word more.

I always consent to experiences of the unexpected. Moreover, the situation offered a unique attraction: the invitation's tone, both familiar and respectful, with those unknown ladies remaining unnamed; its deliberation: "Ah, if you could come!" so vague and so sentimental it seemed suspended over an abyss of confessions, all helped make up my mind. And I arrived with the anxiety of an ineffable emotion. Sometimes in my nightmares, when I recall that fantastic night (with its fantasy made of daily things and its ambiguous mystery growing from the humble root of the possible), it seems to gasp for breath through boulevards of clocks and tall towers solemn as sphinxes pointing toward some Egyptian temple.

The door opened. I was facing the street and suddenly saw a rectangle of light fall on the ground, throwing the shadow of an unknown woman next to mine.

I turned around. With the light behind her blinding my eyes, the woman was only a silhouette to me, on which my imagination could paint various sets of physiognomy, none corresponding to the outline, till I spluttered some greetings and explanations.

"Come in, Alfonso."

Then I stepped in, surprised to hear myself greeted as at

home. The entrance hall was deceptive. The romantic words of the invitation (at least they seemed romantic to me) had given me the hope of coming across an ancient house, full of tapestries, old portraits, and throne-like chairs; an old house without style, but full of respectability. Instead I found myself in a tiny hall with a fragile, graceless staircase, which in turn promised tight, modern proportions in the rest of the house. The floor was of polished wood; the few pieces of furniture had that cold luxury of things from New York, and on the wall, papered in light green, as an unpardonable sign of triviality, two or three Japanese masks grimaced. I even began to doubt. But I raised my eyes and calmed down. Before me, dressed in black, svelte, dignified, the woman who had appeared to greet me showed me to the door of the salon. By now her silhouette had colored in with features; her face would have been insignificant to me, if not for a marked expression of piety. Her brown hair, brushed somewhat carelessly, just then caused a strange conviction in my mind: that her entire being seemed to unfold and form itself on the suggestion of a name.

"Amalia?" I asked.

"Yes." And it seemed to me that I myself had answered.

The living room, as I had imagined, was small. But the furnishings, in answer to my wishes, clashed terribly with the entrance hall. There were the tapestries and great respectable chairs, the bearskin on the floor, the mirror, the fireplace, the decorative vases; the piano full of photographs and tiny statues —the piano played by no one—and, next to the main drawing room, the easel with a larger-than-life portrait (obviously altered) of a gentleman with thick, slack lips and a forked beard.

Doña Magdalena, who was already waiting for me in an enormous red chair, was also dressed in black and wore on her

THE DINNER

breast those hideously large jewels of our parents: a glass ball with a portrait inside, encircled with a gold ring. The mystery of family likeness suddenly absorbed me. My eyes went, unconsciously, from Doña Magdalena to Amalia, and from the portrait to Amalia. Doña Magdalena, who noticed it, aided my study with some timely explanation.

The most appropriate thing would have been to feel uncomfortable, show my surprise, bring about some explanation. But Doña Magdalena and her daughter Amalia hypnotized me, from the first moment, with their parallel glances. Doña Magdalena was a woman of about seventy; thus she consented to leave to her daughter the details of the introduction. Amalia chatted; Doña Magdalena watched me. I was resigned to my fate.

It was up to the mother—according to social custom—to announce the dinner hour. In the dining room the conversation became more general and topical. Eventually I convinced myself that these ladies hadn't wanted anything more than to invite me to dinner, and by the second glass of Chablis I felt immersed in the perfect self-centeredness of a body filled with spiritual generosity. I talked, I laughed, I extolled with all my ingenuity, trying inside to fool myself about the strangeness of my situation. Till that moment the ladies had managed to seem friendly toward me; from then on I felt it was I who was good company to them.

At times the pious air of Amalia's face repeated her mother's face. And the satisfaction, utterly physiological, of Doña Magdalena's face occasionally reverted to her daughter's. It seemed that these two motifs floated in the ambiance, flitting from one face to the other.

I could never have anticipated the pleasures of that conversation. Although she vaguely suggested I don't know what recollections of Sudermann, with frequent recourses to the problematic area of domestic responsibilities and—as was natural in spirited women—sudden Ibsenesque lightning bolts, still I felt as at ease as in the house of some widowed aunt, next to some cousin, a childhood friend now in early stages of spinsterhood.

At first, the conversation centered entirely on matters of trade and economics, with which the two women seemed pleased. There is no better topic when we are invited to dine in some house in which we are not comfortable old friends.

Later, things took another turn. Every phrase began to flit away as if accompanied by some distant request. Each led to an end which even I did not suspect. Eventually there appeared on Amalia's face a sharp, disturbing smile. She began to combat visibly against some internal temptation. Her mouth trembled, at times, with the anxiety of her words, and she always finished with a sigh. Her eyes suddenly dilated, staring with such an expression of fear or abandon on the wall behind me, that more than once, surprised, I even turned around myself. But Amalia seemed unaware of the discomfort that it caused me. She continued with her smiles, her starts and her sighs, so that I shuddered each time her eyes looked over my head.

Finally a real dialogue of sighs began between Amalia and Doña Magdalena. By now I was growing uneasy. Toward the center of the table, and, incidentally, so low that it was a constant annoyance, hung a lamp with two lights. And on the walls it projected the colorless shadows of the two women, in such a way that it was not possible to determine the correspondence between shadows and people. An intense depression came over me, from which I was saved by this unexpected invitation:

"Let's go into the garden."

This new perspective made me regain my spirit. They led me through a room whose spare cleanliness made me think of hospitals. In the dark of the night I could make out a small artificial garden, like that of a church cemetery.

We sat under the trellis. The ladies began to tell me the names of the flowers that I wasn't able to see, relishing the cruel delight of quizzing me afterwards on their recent instruction. My imagination, unsettled by such a long session of eccentricities, found no rest. It scarcely let me listen and almost didn't let me answer. The ladies were now smiling (I guessed as much) in full awareness of my state. I began to mix up their words with my fantasy. Their botanical explanations, when I recall them today, seem as monstrous as delirium: I think I heard them talk of flowers that kiss; of stalks that tear themselves from their roots and climb up your body, like snakes, up to your neck.

The darkness, the weariness, the supper, the Chablis, the mysterious conversation about flowers I couldn't see (and I still don't believe there were any in that stunted garden), were all conducive to sleep; and I fell asleep on the bench, under the trellis.

"Poor captain!" I heard when I opened my eyes. "He left for Europe all full of illusions. For him the lights are extinguished."

In my vicinity the same darkness reigned. A warm breeze made the trellis tremble. Doña Magdalena and Amalia were talking next to me, resigned to my silence. It seemed to me they had exchanged places during my brief sleep; so it seemed to me.

"He was an artillery captain," Amalia told me. "Young and handsome as any."

Her voice wavered.

And at that point something happened that in other circumstances would have seemed natural, but that startled me then and sent my heart to my throat. Until then the ladies had only been perceptible to me by the sensation of their voices and their presence. At that moment someone opened a window in the house, and the light fell unexpectedly on the faces of the women. And—good God!—I saw the faces suddenly lit up, suspended in the air—the black clothing absent in the darkness of the garden—with the expression of piety recorded even in the hardness of their faces. They were like the illuminated faces in the paintings of Echave the Elder, huge and fantastic celestial bodies.

I leaped to my feet before getting control of myself.

"Wait," shouted Doña Magdalena, "the worst is yet to come."

And then, to Amalia:

"My daughter, go on; this gentleman cannot leave us now and go off without hearing it all."

"So then," said Amalia, "the captain left for Europe, he went through Paris at night, he was in such a hurry to get to Berlin. But his greatest wish was to know Paris. In Germany he had to do I don't know what studies in some cannon factory. The day after arriving, he lost his sight in a boiler explosion."

I was going crazy. I tried to ask; what would I ask? I tried to talk; what would I say? What had happened there next to me? Why had they invited me?

The window closed again, and the faces of the women disappeared again. The daughter's voice rang out:

"Oh! Then, and only then, he was taken to Paris. To Paris, which had been his greatest desire. Imagine him going under the Arc d'Étoile, guessing at everything around him . . . But you will speak to him of Paris, won't you? You will talk to him about the Paris he couldn't see. It will do him such good!"

("Ah, if you could make it!" "It will do him such good!")

And then they hauled me to the living room, carrying me by the arms like an invalid. Around my feet the vegetable tendrils had entwined; there were leaves around my head.

"Here he is," they said, showing me a portrait. He was a military man. He was wearing a soldier's helmet, a white cape, with silver stripes on the sleeves like three bugle calls. His beautiful eyes, under the perfect arched eyebrows, had a singular authority. I looked at the women: the two smiled as if relieved after completing a mission. I contemplated the portrait again; I saw myself in the mirror; I verified the similarity: I was like a caricature of that portrait. The portrait had a dedication and a signature. The handwriting was the same as on the unsigned invitation I received that morning.

The portrait had fallen from my hands, and the two women looked at me with comic piety. Something resounded in my ears like a crystal chandelier smashed against the floor.

And I ran through unknown streets. Electric beams danced before my eyes. The clocks on the towers, clogged up with light, were spying on me . . . My God! When I reached the familiar panel of my door, out of breath, the night was shuddering with nine resounding clangs.

On my head were leaves; in my lapel, a modest little flower I had not cut.

Translated by Rick Francis

Tell Them Not to Kill Me!

Juan Rulfo

"Tell them not to kill me, Justino! Go on and tell them that. For God's sake! Tell them. Tell them please for God's sake."

"I can't. There's a sergeant there who doesn't want to hear anything about you."

"Make him listen to you. Use your wits and tell him that scaring me has been enough. Tell him please for God's sake."

"But it's not just to scare you. It seems they really mean to kill you. And I don't want to go back there."

"Go on once more. Just once, to see what you can do."

"No. I don't feel like going. Because if I do they'll know I'm your son. If I keep bothering them they'll end up knowing who I am and will decide to shoot me too. Better leave things the way they are now."

"Go on, Justino. Tell them to take a little pity on me. Just tell them that."

Justino clenched his teeth and shook his head saying no.

And he kept on shaking his head for some time.

"Tell the sergeant to let you see the colonel. And tell him how old I am—how little I'm worth. What will he get out of killing me? Nothing. After all he must have a soul. Tell him to do it for the blessed salvation of his soul."

Justino got up from the pile of stones which he was sitting on and walked to the gate of the corral. Then he turned around to say, "All right. I'll go. But if they decide to shoot me too, who'll take care of my wife and kids?"

"Providence will take care of them, Justino. You go there now and see what you can do for me. That's what matters."

They'd brought him in at dawn. The morning was well along now and he was still there, tied to a post, waiting. He couldn't keep still. He'd tried to sleep for a while to calm down, but he couldn't. He wasn't hungry either. All he wanted was to live. Now that he knew they were really going to kill him, all he could feel was this great desire to stay alive, like a recently resuscitated man.

Who would've thought that old business that happened so long ago and that was buried the way he thought it was would turn up? That business when he had to kill Don Lupe. Not for nothing either, as the people from Alima tried to make out, but because he had his reasons. He remembered: Don Lupe Terreros, the owner of the Puerta de Piedra—and besides that, his *compadre*—was the one he, Juvencio Nava, had to kill, because he'd refused to let him pasture his animals, being the owner of the Puerta de Piedra and his *compadre* too.

At first he didn't do anything because he felt obliged. But later, when the drought came, when he saw how his animals were dying off one by one, plagued by hunger, and how his *compadre* Lupe continued to refuse to let him use his pastures, that was when he began breaking through the fence and driving his herd of skinny animals to the pasture where they could get their fill of grass. And Don Lupe didn't like it and ordered the fence mended, so he, Juvencio Nava, had to cut open the hole again. So, during the day the hole was stopped up and at night it was opened again, while the stock stayed there right next to the fence, always waiting—his stock that before had lived just smelling the grass without being able to taste it.

And he and Don Lupe argued again and again without coming to any agreement.

Until one day Don Lupe said to him, "Look here, Juvencio, if you let another animal in my pasture, I'll kill it."

And he answered him, "Look here, Don Lupe, it's not my fault that the animals look out for themselves. They're innocent. You'll have to pay for it, if you kill them."

"And he killed one of my yearlings.

"This happened thirty-five years ago in March because in April I was already up in the mountains, running away from the summons. The ten cows I gave the judge didn't do me any good, or the lien on my house either, to pay for getting me out of jail. Still later they used up what was left to pay so they wouldn't keep after me, but they kept after me just the same. That's why I came to live with my son on this other piece of land of mine which is called Palo de Venado. And my son grew up and got married to my daughter-in-law Ignacia and has had eight children now. So it happened a long time ago and ought to be forgotten by now. But I guess it's not.

"I figured then that with about a hundred pesos everything could be fixed up. The dead Don Lupe left just his wife and two little kids still crawling. And his widow died soon afterward too—they say from grief. They took the kids far off to some relatives. So there was nothing to fear from them.

"But the rest of the people took the position that I was still summoned to be tried just to scare me so they could keep on robbing me. Every time someone came to the village they told me, 'There are some strangers in town, Juvencio.'

"And I would take off to the mountains, hiding among the madrone thickets and passing the days with nothing to eat but herbs. Sometimes I had to go out at midnight, as though the dogs were after me. It's been that way my whole life. Not just a year or two. My whole life."

And now they've come for him when he no longer expected anyone, confident that people had forgotten all about it, believing that he'd spent at least his last days peacefully. "At least," he thought, "I'll have some peace in my old age. They'll leave me alone."

He'd clung to this hope with all his heart. That's why it was hard for him to imagine that he'd die like this, suddenly, at this time of life, after having fought so much to ward off death, after having spent his best years running from one place to another because of the alarms, now when his body had become all dried up and leathery from the bad days when he had to be in hiding from everybody.

Hadn't he even let his wife go off and leave him? The day when he learned his wife had left him, the idea of going out in search of her didn't even cross his mind. He let her go without trying to find out at all who she went with or where, so he wouldn't have to go down to the village. He let her go as he'd let everything else go, without putting up a fight. All he had left to take care of was his life, and he'd do that, if nothing else. He couldn't let them kill him. He couldn't. Much less now.

But that's why they brought him from there, from Palo de Venado. They didn't need to tie him so he'd follow them. He walked alone, tied by his fear. They realized he couldn't run with his old body, with those skinny legs of his like dry bark, cramped up with the fear of dying. Because that's where he was headed. For death. They told him so.

That's when he knew. He began to feel that stinging in his stomach that always came on suddenly when he saw death nearby making his eyes big with fear and his mouth swell up with those mouthfuls of sour water he had to swallow unwillingly.

And that thing that made his feet heavy while his head felt soft and his heart pounded with all its force against his ribs. No, he couldn't get used to the idea that they were going to kill him.

There must be some hope. Somewhere there must still be some hope left. Maybe they'd made a mistake. Perhaps they were looking for another Juvencio Nava and not him.

He walked along in silence between those men, with his arms fallen at his sides. The early morning hour was dark, starless. The wind blew slowly, whipping the dry earth back and forth, which was filled with that odor like urine that dusty roads have.

His eyes, which had become squinty with the years, were looking down at the ground, here under his feet, in spite of the darkness. There in the earth was his whole life. Sixty years of living on it, of holding it tight in his hands, of tasting it like one tastes the flavor of meat. For a long time he'd been crumbling it with his eyes, savoring each piece as if it were the last one, almost knowing it would be the last.

Then, as if wanting to say something, he looked at the men who were marching along next to him. He was going to tell them to let him loose, to let him go: "I haven't hurt anybody, boys," he was going to say to them, but he kept silent. "A little further on I'll tell them," he thought. And he just looked at them. He could even imagine they were his friends, but he didn't want to. They weren't. He didn't know who they were. He watched them moving at his side and bending down from time to time to see where the road continued.

He'd seen them for the first time at nightfall, that dusky hour when everything seems scorched. They'd crossed the furrows treading on the tender corn. And he'd gone down there to tell them that the corn was beginning to grow. But that didn't stop them.

He'd seen them in time. He'd always had the luck to see everything in time. He could've hidden, gone up in the mountains for a few hours until they left, and then come down again. Already it was time for the rains to have come, but the rains didn't come and the corn was beginning to wither. Soon it'd be all dried up.

So it hadn't even been worthwhile, his going down and placing himself among those men like in a hole, never to get out again.

And now he continued beside them, holding back how he wanted to tell them to let him go. He didn't see their faces, he only saw their bodies, which swung toward him and then away from him. So when he started talking he didn't know if they'd heard him. He said, "I've never hurt anybody." That's what he said. But nothing changed. Not one of the bodies seemed to pay attention. The faces didn't turn to look at him. They kept right on, as if they were walking in their sleep.

Then he thought that there was nothing else he could say, that he would have to look for hope somewhere else. He let his arms fall again to his sides and went by the first houses of the village, among those four men, darkened by the black color of the night.

"Colonel, here is the man."

They'd stopped in front of the narrow doorway. He stood with his hat in his hand, respectfully, waiting to see someone come out. But only the voice came out, "What man?"

"The one from Palo de Venado, Colonel. The one you ordered us to bring in."

"Ask him if he ever lived in Alima," came the voice from inside again.

"Hey, you. Ever lived in Alima?" the sergeant facing him repeated the question.

"Yes. Tell the colonel that's where I'm from. And that I lived there till not long ago."

"Ask him if he knew Guadalupe Terreros."

"He says did you know Guadalupe Terreros?"

"Don Lupe? Yes. Tell him that I knew him. He's dead."

Then the voice inside changed tone: "I know he died," it said. And the voice continued talking, as if it was conversing with someone there on the other side of the reed wall.

"Guadalupe Terreros was my father. When I grew up and looked for him they told me he was dead. It's hard to grow up knowing that the thing we have to hang on to, to take roots from, is dead. That's what happened to us.

"Later on I learned that he was killed by being hacked first with a machete and then an oxgoad stuck in his belly. They told me he lasted more than two days and that when they found him, lying in an arroyo, he was still in agony and begging that his family be taken care of.

"As time goes by you seem to forget this. You try to forget it. What you can't forget is finding out that the one who did it is still alive, feeding his rotten soul with the illusion of eternal life. I couldn't forgive that man, even though I don't know him; but the fact that I know where he is makes me want to finish him off. I can't forgive his still living. He should never have been born."

From here, from outside, all he said was clearly heard. Then he ordered, "Take him and tie him up awhile, so he'll suffer and then shoot him!"

"Look at me, Colonel!" he begged. "I'm not worth anything now. It won't be long before I die all by myself, crippled by old age. Don't kill me!"

"Take him away!" repeated the voice from inside.

"I've already paid, Colonel. I've paid many times over. They took everything away from me. They punished me in many ways. I've spent about forty years hiding like a leper, always with the fear they'd kill me at any moment. I don't deserve to die like this, Colonel. Let the Lord pardon me, at least. Don't kill me! Tell them not to kill me!"

There he was, as if they'd beaten him, waving his hat against the ground. Shouting.

Immediately the voice from inside said, "Tie him up and give him something to drink until he gets drunk so the shots won't hurt him."

Finally, now, he'd been quieted. There he was, slumped down at the foot of the post. His son Justino had come and his son Justino had gone and had returned and now was coming again.

He slung him on top of the burro. He cinched him up tight against the saddle so he wouldn't fall off on the road. He put his head in a sack so it wouldn't give such a bad impression. And then he made the burro giddap, and away they went in a hurry to reach Palo de Venado in time to arrange the wake for the dead man.

"Your daughter-in-law and grandchildren will miss you," he was saying to him. "They'll look at your face and won't believe it's you. They'll think the coyote has been eating on you when they see your face full of holes from all those bullets they shot at you."

Translated by George D. Schade

The Carnival of the Bullets

Martín Luis Guzmán

My interest in Villa[1] and his activities often made me ask myself, while I was in Ciudad Juárez, which exploits would best paint the Division of the North: those supposed to be strictly historical or those rated as legendary; those related exactly as they had been seen, or those in which a touch of poetic fancy brought out their essence more clearly. These second always seemed to me truer, more worthy of being considered history.

For instance, where could one find a better painting of Rodolfo Fierro[2]—and Fierro and Villa's movement were two facing mirrors that reflected each other endlessly—than in the account of how he carried out the terrible orders of his chief after one of the battles, revealing an imagination as cruel as it was fertile in death devices? This vision of him left in the soul the sensation of a reality so overwhelming that the memory of it lives forever.

That battle, which was successful in every way, had left not less than five hundred prisoners in Villa's hands. Villa ordered them to be divided into two groups: the Orozco volunteers,

[1] *Villa*: Pancho Villa (1878-1923) was a general and folk hero in the Mexican Revolution who led the Division of the North.

[2] *Rodolfo Fierro*: "the executioner," a lieutenant in the army of Pancho Villa during the Mexican Revolution.

whom we called "Reds," in one, and the Federals[3] in the other. And as he felt himself strong enough to take extreme measures, he decided to make an example of the first group and to act more generously toward the second. The "Reds" were to be executed before dark; the Federals were to be given their choice of joining the revolutionary troops or returning home, after promising not to take up arms again against the Constitutionalist[4] cause.

Fierro, as might have been expected, was put in charge of the execution, and he displayed in it that efficiency which was already winning him great favor with Villa, his "chief," as he called him.

It was growing late in the afternoon. The revolutionary forces, off duty, were slowly gathering in the little village that had been the objective of their offensive. The cold, penetrating wind of the Chihuahuan plains began to blow up, and the groups of cavalry and infantry sought protection against the groups of buildings. But Fierro—whom nothing and nobody ever held back—was not to be put out by a cool breeze that at most meant frost that night. He cantered along on his horse, whose dark coat was still covered with the dust of battle. The wind was blowing in his face, but he neither buried his chin in his breast nor raised the folds of his blanket around his face. He carried his head high, his chest thrown out, his feet firm in the stirrups, and his legs gracefully flexed under the campaign equipment that hung from the saddle straps. The barren plain and an occasional soldier that passed at a distance were his only spectators. But he, perhaps without even thinking about

[3] *Federals*: soldiers in the Mexican army.

[4] *Constitutionalist*: the Constitutionalists were a faction of the Mexican Revolution that dominated politics from the revolution until the late 1970s, made up mainly of the middle-class, liberals, and intellectuals dedicated to a constitution based on the idea of "Mexico for Mexicans."

MARTÍN LUIS GUZMÁN

it, reined his horse to make him show his gaits as though he were on parade. Fierro was happy; the satisfaction of victory filled his being; and to him victory was complete only when it meant the utter rout of the enemy; and in this frame of mind even the buffeting of the wind, and riding after fifteen hours in the saddle, were agreeable. The rays of the pale setting sun seemed to caress him as they fell.

He reached the stableyard where the condemned prisoners were shut up like a herd of cattle, and he reined in a moment to look at them over the fence rails. They were well-built men of the type of Chihuahua, tall, compact, with strong necks and well-set-up shoulders on vigorous, flexible backs. As Fierro looked over the little captive army and sized up its military value and prowess, a strange pulsation ran through him, a twitching that went from his heart or from his forehead out to the index finger of his right hand. Involuntarily the palm of this hand reached out to the butt of his pistol.

"Here's a battle for you," he thought.

The cavalrymen, bored with their task of guarding the prisoners, paid no attention to him. The only thing that mattered to them was the annoyance of mounting this tiresome guard, all the worse after the excitement of the battle. They had to have their rifles ready on their knees, and when an occasional soldier left the group, they aimed at him with an air that left no room for doubt as to their intentions, and, if necessary, fired. A wave would run over the formless surface of the mass of the prisoners, who huddled together to avoid the shot. The bullet either went wide or shot one of them down.

Fierro rode up to the gate of the stableyard. He called to a soldier, who let down the bars, and went in. Without taking off his serape he dismounted. His legs were numb with cold and weariness, and he stretched them. He settled his two pistols in their holsters. Next he began to look slowly over the pens, observing their layout and how they were divided up. He took several steps over to one of the fences, where he tied his horse to a fence board. He slipped something out of one of the pockets of his saddle into his coat pocket and crossed the yard, at a short distance from the prisoners.

There were three pens that opened into one another, with gates and a narrow passageway between. From the one where the prisoners were kept, Fierro went into the middle enclosure, slipping through the bars of the gate. He went straight over to the next one. There he stopped. His tall, handsome figure seemed to give off a strange radiance, something superior, awe-inspiring, and yet not out of keeping with the desolation of the barnyard. His serape had slipped down until it barely hung from his shoulders; the tassels of the corners dragged on the ground. His gray, broad-brimmed hat turned rose-colored where the slanting rays of the setting sun fell on it. Through the fences the prisoners could see him at a distance, his back turned toward them. His legs formed a pair of herculean, glistening compasses: it was the gleam of his leather puttees in the light of the afternoon.

About a hundred yards away, outside the pens, was the officer of the troop in charge of the prisoners. Fierro made signs to him to come closer, and the officer rode over to the fence beside Fierro. The two began to talk. In the course of the conversation Fierro pointed out different spots in the enclosure in which he was standing and in the one next to it. Then he described with gestures of his hand a series of operations, which the officer repeated, as though to understand them better, Fierro repeated two or three times what seemed to be a very important operation, and the officer, now sure about his orders, galloped off toward the prisoners.

Fierro turned back toward the center of the stableyard, studying once more the layout of the fence, and other details. That pen was the largest of the three, and the first in order, the nearest to the town. On two sides gates opened into the fields; the bars of these, though more worn than those of the farther pens, were of better wood. On the other side there was a gate that opened into the adjoining pen, and on the far side the fence was not of boards, but was an adobe wall, not less than six feet high. The wall was about one hundred and thirty feet long, and about forty feet of it formed the back of a shed or stall, the roof of which sloped down from the wall and rested on the one side on the end posts of the lateral fence, which had been left longer, and on the other on a wall, also of adobe, which came out perpendicular from the wall and extended some twenty-five feet into the barnyard. Thus, between the shed and the fence of the adjoining lot, there was a space enclosed on two sides by solid walls. In that corner the wind that afternoon was piling up rubbish and clanging an iron bucket against the well-curb with an arbitrary rhythm. From the well-curb there rose up two rough forked posts, crossed by a third, from which a pulley and chain hung, which also rattled in the wind. On the tip of one of the forks sat a large whitish bird, hardly distinguishable from the twisted points of the dry pole.

Fierro was standing about fifty steps from the well. He rested his eye for a moment on the motionless bird, and as though its presence fitted in perfectly with his thoughts, without a change of attitude or expression, he slowly pulled out his pistol. The long, polished barrel of the gun turned into a glowing finger in the light of the sun. Slowly it rose until it pointed in the direction of the bird. A shot rang out—dry and diminutive in the immensity of the afternoon—and the bird dropped to the ground. Fierro returned his pistol to its holster.

At that moment a soldier jumped over the fence into the yard. It was Fierro's orderly. It had been such a high jump that it took him several seconds to get to his feet. When he finally did, he walked over to where his master was standing.

Without turning his head Fierro asked:

"What about them? If they don't come soon, we aren't going to have time."

"I think they're coming."

"Then you hurry up and get over there. Let's see, what pistol have you got?"

"The one you gave me, chief. The Smith and Wesson."

"Hand it over here and take these boxes of bullets. How many bullets have you got?"

"I gathered up about fifteen dozen today, chief. Some of the others found lots of them, but I didn't."

"Fifteen dozen? I told you the other day that if you kept on selling ammunition to buy booze, I'd put a bullet through you."

"No, chief."

"What do you mean: 'No, chief'?"

"I do get drunk, chief, but I don't sell the ammunition."

"Well, you watch out, for you know me. And now you move lively so this stunt will be a success. I fire and you load the pistols. And mind what I tell you: if on your account a single one of the Reds gets away, I'll put you to sleep with them."

"Oh, chief!"

"You heard what I said."

The orderly spread his blanket on the ground and emptied onto it the boxes of cartridges that Fierro had just given him. Then he began to take out one by one the bullets in his cartridge belt. He was in such a hurry that it took him longer than it should have. He was so nervous that his fingers seemed all thumbs.

"What a chief!" he kept thinking to himself.

In the meantime, behind the fence of the adjoining barn lot, soldiers of the guard began to appear. They were on horseback, and their shoulders showed above the top fence rail. There were many others along the two other fences.

Fierro and his orderly were the only ones inside the barnyard; Fierro stood with a pistol in his hand, and his serape fallen at his feet. His orderly squatted beside him lining up the bullets in rows on his blanket.

The commander of the troop rode up through the gate that opened into the next lot, and said:

"I've got the first ten ready. Shall I let them out for you?"

"Yes," answered Fierro, "but first explain things to them. As soon as they come through the gate, I'll begin to shoot. Those that reach the wall and get over it are free. If anyone of them doesn't want to come through, you put a bullet into him."

The officer went back the same way, and Fierro, pistol in hand, stood attentive, his eyes riveted on the narrow space through which the soldiers had to come out. He stood close enough to the dividing fence so that, as he fired, the bullets would not hit the Reds who were still on the other side. He wanted to keep his promise faithfully. But he was not so close that the prisoners could not see, the minute they came through the gate, the pistol that was leveled at them twenty paces off. Behind Fierro the setting sun turned the sky into a fiery ball. The wind kept blowing.

In the barnyard where the prisoners were herded, the voices grew louder, but the howling of the wind made the shouts sound like herders rounding up cattle, it was a hard task to make the three hundred condemned men pass from the last to the middle lot. At the thought of the torture awaiting them, the whole group writhed with the convulsions of a person in the grip of hysteria. The soldiers of the guard shouted, and every minute the reports of the rifles seemed to emphasize the screams as with a whip crack.

Out of the first prisoners that reached the middle pen a group of soldiers separated ten. There were at least twenty-five soldiers. They spurred their horses on to the prisoners to make them move; they rested the muzzles of their rifles against their bodies.

"Traitors! Dirty bastards! Let's see you run and jump. Get a move on, you traitor!"

And in this way they made them advance to the gate where Fierro and his orderly were waiting. Here the resistance of the Reds grew stronger; but the horses' hooves and the gun barrels persuaded them to choose the other danger, the danger of Fierro, which was not an inch away, but twenty paces.

As soon as they appeared within his range of vision, Fierro greeted them with a strange phrase, at once cruel and affectionate, half ironical and half encouraging.

"Come on, boys; I'm only going to shoot, and I'm a bad shot."

The prisoners jumped like goats. The first one tried to throw himself on Fierro, but he had not made three bounds before he fell, riddled by bullets from the soldiers stationed along the fence. The others ran as fast as they could toward the wall—a mad race that must have seemed to them like a dream. One tried to take refuge behind the well-curb: he was the target for Fierro's first bullet. The others fell as they ran, one by one; in less than ten seconds Fierro had fired eight times, and the last of the group dropped just as his fingers were touching the adobe that by the strange whim of the moment separated the zone of life from the zone of death. Some of the bodies showed signs of life; the soldiers finished them off from their horses.

And then came another group of ten, and then another, and another, and another. The three pistols of Fierro—his two and that of his orderly—alternated with precise rhythm in the homicidal hand. Six shots from each one, six shots fired without stopping to aim and without pause, and then the gun dropped on to the orderly's blanket, where he removed the exploded caps, and reloaded it. Then, without changing his position, he held out the pistol to Fierro, who took it as he let the other fall. Through the orderly's fingers passed the bullets that seconds later would leave the prisoners stretched lifeless, but he did not raise his eyes to see those that fell. His whole soul seemed concentrated on the pistol in his hand, and on the bullets, with their silver and burnished reflections, spread out on the ground before him. Just two sensations filled his whole being: the cold weight of the bullets that he was putting into the openings of the barrel, and the warm smoothness of the gun. Over his head one after another rang out the shots of his "chief," entertaining himself with his sharpshooting.

The panic-stricken flight of the prisoners toward the wall of salvation—a fugue of death in which the two themes of the passion to kill and the infinite desire to live were blended— lasted almost two hours.

Not for one minute did Fierro lose his precision of aim or his poise. He was firing at moving human targets, targets that jumped and slipped in pools of blood and amidst corpses stretched out in unbelievable postures, but he fired without other emotion than that of hitting or missing. He calculated the deflection caused by the wind, and corrected it with each shot.

Some of the prisoners, crazed by terror, fell to their knees as they came through the gate. There the bullet laid them low. Others danced about grotesquely behind the shelter of the well-curb until the bullet cured them of their frenzy or they dropped wounded into the well. But nearly all rushed toward the adobe wall and tried to climb it over the warm, damp, steaming heaps of piled-up bodies. Some managed to dig their nails into the earth coping, but their hands, so avid of life, soon fell lifeless.

There came a moment in which the mass execution became a noisy tumult, punctuated by the dry snap of the pistol shots, muted by the voice of the wind. On one side of the fence the shouts of those who fled from death only to die; on the other, those who resisted the pressure of the horsemen and tried to break through the wall that pushed them on toward that terrible gate. And to the shouts of one group and the other were added the voices of the soldiers stationed along the fences. The noise of the shooting, the marksmanship of Fierro, and the cries and frantic gestures of the condemned men had worked them up to a pitch of great excitement. The somersaults of the bodies as they fell in the death agony elicited loud exclamations of amusement from them, and they shouted, gesticulated, and gave peals of laughter as they fired into the mounds of bodies in which they saw the slightest evidence of life.

In the last squad of victims there were twelve instead of ten. The twelve piled out of the death pen, falling over one another, each trying to protect himself with the others, in his anxiety to win in the horrible race. To go forward they had to jump over the piled-up corpses, but not for this reason did the bullet err in its aim. With sinister precision it hit them one by one and left them on the way to the wall, arms and legs outstretched, embracing the mass of their motionless companions. But one of them, the only one left alive, managed to reach the coping and swing himself over. The firing stopped and the troop of soldiers crowded into the corner of the adjoining barn lot to see the fugitive.

It was beginning to get dark. It took the soldiers a little while to focus their vision in the twilight. At first they could see nothing. Finally, far off, in the vastness of the darkling plain they managed to make out a moving spot. As it ran, the body bent so far over that it almost seemed to crawl along on the ground.

A soldier took aim. "It's hard to see," he said as he fired. The report died away in the evening wind. The moving spot fled on.

Fierro had not moved from his place. His arm was exhausted, and he let it hang limp against his side for a long time. Then he became aware of a pain in his forefinger and raised his hand to his face; he could see that the finger was somewhat swollen. He rubbed it gently between the fingers and the palm of his other hand and for a good space of time kept up this gentle massage. Finally he stooped over and picked up his serape, which he had taken off at the beginning of the executions. He threw it over his shoulders and walked to the shelter of the stalls. But after a few steps he turned to his orderly:

"When you're finished, bring up the horses."

And he went on his way.

The orderly was gathering up the exploded caps. In the next pen the soldiers of the guard had dismounted and were talking or singing softly. The orderly heard them in silence and without raising his head. Finally he got slowly to his feet. He gathered up the blanket by the four corners and threw it over his shoulder. The empty caps rattled in it with a dull tintinnabulation.

It was dark. A few stars glimmered, and on the other side of the fence the cigarettes shone red. The orderly walked heavily and slowly and, half feeling his way, went to the last of the pens and in a little while returned leading his own and his master's horses by the bridle; across one of his shoulders swung the haversack.

He made his way over to the stalls. Fierro was sitting on a rock, smoking. The wind whistled through the cracks in the boards.

"Unsaddle the horse and make up my bed," ordered Fierro. "I'm so tired I can't stand up."

"Here in this pen, chief? Here?"

"Sure. Why not?"

The orderly did as he was ordered. He unsaddled the horse and spread the blankets on the straw, making a kind of pillow out of the haversack and the saddle. Fierro stretched out and in a few minutes was asleep.

The orderly lighted his lantern and bedded the horses for the night. Then he blew out the light, wrapped himself in his blanket, and lay down at the feet of his master. But in a minute he was up again and knelt down and crossed himself. Then he stretched out on the straw again.

Six or seven hours went by. The wind had died down. The silence of the night was bathed in moonlight. Occasionally a horse snuffled. The radiance of the moon gleamed on the dented surface of the bucket that hung by the well and made clear shadows of all the objects in the yard except the mounds of corpses. These rose up, enormous in the stillness of the night, like fantastic hills, strange and confused in outline.

The blue silver of the night descended on the corpses in rays of purest light. But little by little that light turned into a voice, a voice that had the unreality of the night. It grew distinct; it was a voice that was barely audible, faint and tortured, but clear like the shadows cast by the moon. From the center of one of the mounds of corpses the voice seemed to whisper:

"Oh! Oh!"

The heaped-up bodies, stiff and cold for hours, lay motionless in the barnyard. The moonlight sank into them as into an inert mass. But the voice sounded again:

"Oh . . . Oh . . . Oh . . . "

And this last groan reached to the spot where Fierro's orderly lay sleeping and brought him out of sleep to the consciousness of hearing. The first thing that came to his mind was the memory of the execution of the three hundred prisoners; the mere thought of it kept him motionless in the straw, his eyes half open and his whole soul fixed on the lamentation of that voice:

"Oh . . . please . . . "

Fierro tossed on his bed.

"Please . . . water . . . "

Fierro awoke and listened attentively.

"Please . . . water . . . "

Fierro stretched out his foot until he touched his orderly.

"Hey, you. Don't you hear? One of those dead men is asking for water."

"Yes, chief."

"You get up and put a bullet through the sniveling son of a bitch. Let's see if he'll let me get some sleep then."

"A bullet through who, chief?"

"The one that's asking for water, you fool. Don't you understand?"

"Water, please," the voice kept on.

The orderly took his pistol from under the saddle and started out of the shed in search of the voice. He shivered with fear and cold. He felt sick to his soul.

He looked around in the light of the moon. Everybody he

touched was stiff. He hesitated without knowing what to do. Finally he fired in the direction from which the voice came. The voice kept on. The orderly fired again. The voice died away.

The moon floated through the limitless space of its blue light. Under the shelter of the shed Fierro slept.

Translated by Harriet de Onís

Permission Granted

EDMUNDO VALADÉS

The engineers converse up on stage. They laugh. They go at each other with raw humor. They let fly with off-color jokes, the kind with invariably barbed punch lines. Little by little, their focus shifts to the auditorium. They stop reminiscing over their last bender, or exchanging confidences about the girl who just debuted in the house of ill repute where they're regulars. Now the subject of their conversation turns to these men down below, all of these peasants assembled here before them.

"That's right, we should be redeeming them. They've got to be incorporated into our civilization: cleaned up on the outside, taught to be dirty on the inside."

"You, sir, are a skeptic. Moreover, you're casting judgment upon our efforts, the Revolution's efforts."

"Bah! What's the point? These poor bastards are beyond redemption. They're rotten with alcohol, ignorance. Distributing land among them hasn't done any good."

"My esteemed colleague, you're both superficial and a defeatist. We're the ones to blame. We've given them land, and now what? We're very pleased with ourselves. But what about credit, installments, new agricultural technology, machinery, how are they supposed to come up with all of that?"

The chairman, twirling his thick moustache, a well-stroked flagpole on which his fingers are raised with pleasure, watches from behind his spectacles, immune to the engineers' verbal fencing. Whenever the earthy, spicy, animal smell of the men accommodated on the benches tickles his nose, he takes out his bandana and blows it noisily. He was also a man of the fields once. But that was a long time ago. Now, after the city and his office, all that's left are the handkerchief and the roughness of his hands.

The men down there below are solemnly seated, with all the reserve of a farmer who has entered a closed chamber: an assembly, or a church. They don't have much to say, and the words they do exchange refer to harvests, rain, animals, credit. Many of them carry bundles of food at their shoulders, magazines to combat their hunger with. Some of them smoke cigarettes that seem to have grown out of their own hands in a calm, leisurely fashion.

Others are on foot, leaning against the walls on either side with their arms crossed over their chests, tranquilly standing guard.

The chairman rings his little bell, and its jingle dispels their murmurs. The engineers begin. They speak of agrarian issues, the need to increase production and improve crops. They promise aid to the parcel owners, then encourage them to voice their needs.

"We want to help you, you can trust us."

Now, it's the turn of the men down below. The chairman invites them to present their concerns. One hand is timidly raised. Others follow. They discuss what matters to them: water, local bosses, credit, schools. Some are direct, precise; others get confused and can't seem to express themselves. They scratch their heads and turn their faces to search for whatever it was they were going to say, as if their idea were hiding from them in some corner, or in another comrade's eyes, or up there where the chandelier is hanging.

Over there, in one group, there's whispering. They're all from the same town. Some grave matter is bothering them. They consult one another, mulling over who should speak for them.

"I'm considering Jilipe: he sure knows lots."

"C'mon, how about you, Juan, you spoke last time."

There's no consensus. The men being discussed wait to see if they'll be pushed into it. Then an old man, the patriarch perhaps, decides:

"Well, how about giving Sacramento a try."

Sacramento waits.

"Go on, now, raise your hand."

The hand is raised, but the chairman doesn't see it. Others are more visible and have taken his chance. Sacramento searches the old man's face. Another, very young man raises his hand high in the air. Five dark, dirty fingers can be seen above the forest of shaggy heads. The hand is discovered by the president. Now he has the floor.

"All right, stand up, then."

The hand is lowered once Sacramento gets to his feet. He tries to find a place for his hat. The hat has become a wide nuisance, it's grown bigger, it doesn't seem to fit anywhere. In the end, Sacramento continues holding it in his hands. There are signs of impatience from the table. Then the president's voice jumps out, authoritarian, menacing:

"You there, the one who asked to speak, we're waiting."

Sacramento fixes his gaze on the engineer over at one end of the table. It would seem he's going to address only him; as if the rest had disappeared, and only the two of them remained in the hall.

"I'd like to speak for all of us from San Juan de las Manzanas. We've got a complaint against the municipal president. He's been giving us a lot of trouble, and we can't take any more. First, he took away Felipe Pérez and Juan Hernández's parcels of land, because they were right next to his. We telegraphed Mexico City and they didn't even answer us. The members of the assembly got to talking, and we thought it was a good idea to go to the Agrarians for some restitution. 'Cause all that runaround and paperwork didn't do no good, the municipal president kept that land anyhow."

Sacramento speaks without any visible emotion. You might think he was reciting an old prayer, one he knows by heart, from beginning to end.

"So anyway, since he figured we had it in for him, he accused us of so-called unrest. You'd think we'd taken his land away. Then here he comes with this business about accounts: yessir, loans, he said we were supposedly falling behind. And the agent shared his wrong thinking, so we had to pay all sorts of interest. Crescencio, the man who lives near the hill, over yonder where the drainage is, understands something about this numbers business. Well, he did the math and it just wasn't so, they were trying to overcharge us. But the municipal president brought in some gentlemen from Mexico City with all their legal mumbo jumbo, and if we didn't pay up, they were gonna take our land. So you might say he was charging us by force for what we never owed."

Sacramento speaks without emphasis, without premeditated pauses. It's as if he were plowing the earth. His words fall like grains being sowed.

"And then there was that business about my boy. Yessir, he got all riled up. And you better believe he gave me a bad feeling. I tried to stop him. But he'd been drinking, and his head was all scrambled. Having respect for me meant nothing to him. He went out looking for the municipal president, to protest . . . And they killed him, just like that, 'cause he was trying to steal a cow from the municipal president, or so they say. They brought him back to me dead, his face a wreck."

Sacramento's Adam's apple trembles. No more than that. He's still standing, like a tree clinging to its roots. Nothing more. His gaze is still fixed on the same engineer, seated down at one end of the table.

"Then there's the water. Since there wasn't much to be had, because the rains were no good, the municipal president closed the canal. And since the cornfields were gonna dry out and the assembly was gonna have a bad year, we went looking for him to ask could he spare a little water for our crops, yessir. And he received us so poorly, it looked like he was really going to lose his temper. Stubborn as a mule, just so he could do us more damage."

A hand pulls at Sacramento's arm. One of his companions points out something else to him. Sacramento's voice is the only one that echoes in the chamber.

"And as if that weren't enough, that business about the water, I mean—because thank the Virgencita, we got some more rain and salvaged half the harvests—there's what happened last Saturday. The municipal president and his men, who are really bad news, they up and took two of our girls: Lupita, who was engaged to marry Herminio, and Crescencio's daughter. Since they caught us unawares, while we were busy with our chores, we couldn't do nothing to stop them. They forced them to go up on the mountain, then left them lying there. And we didn't have to ask no questions 'cause by the time those girls got back, they were in pretty bad shape: they went so far as to beat them. And then the people really got up in arms, since we're sick and tired of being at the mercy of such rotten authorities."

For the first time, Sacramento's voice vibrated. A threat, hatred, an ominous decision were all pulsating in it.

"So, since no one pays us any mind, by that I mean all those authorities we went to, and who knows if justice will ever be done, we'd like to take some precautions here. You—"and now, Sacramento marks every engineer in turn with his gaze, holding it upon reaching the man who presides over the table, "—who've promised to help us, give us your dispensation to punish the municipal president of San Juan de las Manzanas. We're asking your leave to take justice into our own hands."

All eyes are glued on the men up on the platform. The chairman and the engineers, dumbfounded, exchange looks. Finally, they discuss the matter.

"This is absurd. We can't sanction such an unthinkable request."

"No, my esteemed colleague, it isn't at all absurd. What's truly absurd is leaving this matter in the hands of men who haven't done anything, who've turned a deaf ear to those voices. It would be cowardly to wait for our justice system to do them justice; they'd never believe in us again. I prefer to be on the side of these men. Their justice is primitive, but it is justice in the end; I'll assume alongside them my share of responsibility. As far as I'm concerned, we've got no choice but to give them what they want."

"But we're civilized, we have institutions, we can't just push them aside."

"It would justify barbarity, acting outside the law."

"And what worse acts are there outside the law than the ones they're denouncing? If we'd been offended like they have; if we'd suffered less harm than they have, we'd have already forgotten about whether justice should intervene or not. I demand that this proposal be subject to a vote."

"I feel the same way you do, comrade."

"But you know how crafty their kind is. We ought to look

into what really happened. Besides, we don't have the authority to grant a request like this."

And now the chairman intervenes. The man of the fields has risen up in him. His voice brooks no appeal.

"Let the assembly decide. I'll assume full responsibility."

He addresses the auditorium. His voice is a farmer's voice, the same voice he must have used once to speak up in the sierra, the kind that blends in with the earth, with his people.

"The proposal by our companions from San Juan de las Manzanas will now be put to a vote. All those who agree that they should be authorized to kill the municipal president, raise your hands."

Every arm is stretched high. There isn't a single hand that isn't up in the air, categorically approving the measure, including the engineers'. Every finger pointing directly towards summary execution.

"The assembly grants the party from San Juan de las Manzanas permission for their request."

Then Sacramento, who has remained standing, calm, finishes speaking. There is no joy or pain in what he says. His expression is plain, simple.

"Well now, thanks very kindly for the permission, because since no one would listen to us, as of yesterday, the municipal president of San Juan de las Manzanas is dead."

Translated by Tanya Huntington

PERMISSION GRANTED

THE UNEXPECTED

IN EVERYDAY, URBAN LIFE

The Shunammite

INÉS ARREDONDO

*So they sought for a fair damsel throughout all the coasts of Israel,
and found Abishag a Shunammite, and brought her to the king.
And the damsel was very fair, and cherished the king, and
ministered to him: but the king knew her not.*

I Kings I:3-4

The summer had been a fiery furnace. The last summer of my youth.

Tense, concentrated in the arrogance that precedes combustion, the city shone in a dry and dazzling light. I stood in the very midst of the light, dressed in mourning, proud, feeding the flames with my blonde hair, alone. Men's sly glances slid over my body without soiling it, and my haughty modesty forced them to barely nod at me, full of respect. I was certain of having the power to dominate passions, to purify anything in the scorching air that surrounded but did not singe me.

Nothing changed when I received the telegram; the sadness it brought me did not affect in the least my feelings towards the world. My uncle Apolonio was dying at the age of seventy-odd years and wanted to see me. I had lived as a daughter in his house for many years and I sincerely felt pain at the thought of his inevitable death. All this was perfectly normal, and not a single omen, not a single shiver made me suspect anything. Quickly I made arrangements for the journey, in the very same untouchable midst of the motionless summer.

I arrived at the village during the hour of siesta.

Walking down the empty streets with my small suitcase, I fell to daydreaming, in that dusky zone between reality and time, born of the excessive heat. I was not remembering; I was almost reliving things as they had been. "Look, Licha, the *amapas* are blooming again." The clear voice, almost childish. "I want you to get yourself a dress like that of Margarita Ibarra to wear on the sixteenth." I could hear her, feel her walking by my side, her shoulders bent a little forwards, light in spite of her plumpness, happy and old. I carried on walking in the company of my aunt Panchita, my mother's sister. "Well, my dear, if you *really* don't like Pepe . . . but he's such a *nice* boy." Yes, she had used those exact words, here, in front of Tichi Valenzuela's window, with her gay smile, innocent and impish. I walked a little further, where the paving stones seemed to fade away in the haze, and when the bells rang, heavy and real, ending the siesta and announcing the Rosary, I opened my eyes and gave the village a good, long look: it was not the same. The *amapas* had not bloomed and I was crying, in my mourning dress, at the door of my uncle's house.

The front gate was open, as always, and at the end of the courtyard rose the bougainvillea. As always: but not the same. I dried my tears, and felt that I was not arriving: I was leaving. Everything looked motionless, pinioned in my memory, and the heat and the silence seemed to wither it all. My footsteps echoed with a new sound, and María came out to greet me.

"Why didn't you let us know? We'd have sent . . . "

We went straight into the sick man's room. As I entered, I felt cold. Silence and gloom preceded death.

"Luisa, is that you?"

The dear voice was dying out and would soon be silent for ever.

"I'm here, uncle."

"God be praised! I won't die alone."

"Don't say that; you'll soon be much better."

He smiled sadly; he knew I was lying but he did not want to make me cry.

"Yes, my daughter. Yes. Now have a rest, make yourself at home and then come and keep me company. I'll try to sleep a little."

Shriveled, wizened, toothless, lost in the immense bed and floating senselessly in whatever was left of his life, he was painful to be with, like something superfluous, out of place, like so many others at the point of death. Stepping out of the over-heated passageway, one would take a deep breath, instinctively, hungry for light and air.

I began to nurse him and I felt happy doing it. This house was *my* house, and in the morning, while tidying up, I would sing long-forgotten songs. The peace that surrounded me came perhaps from the fact that my uncle no longer awaited death as something imminent and terrible, but instead let himself be carried by the passing days towards a more or less distant or nearby future, with the unconscious tenderness of a child. He would go over his past life with great pleasure and enjoy imagining that he was bequeathing me his images, as grandparents do with their children.

"Bring me that small chest, there, in the large wardrobe. Yes, that one. The key is underneath the mat, next to Saint Anthony. Bring the key as well."

And his sunken eyes would shine once again at the sight of all his treasures.

"Look: this necklace—I gave it to your aunt for our tenth wedding anniversary. I bought it in Mazatlán from a Polish jeweler who told me God-knows-what story about an Austrian princess, and asked an impossible price for it. I brought it back hidden in my pistol-holder and didn't sleep a wink in the stagecoach—I was so afraid someone would steal it!"

THE SHUNAMMITE

The light of dusk made the young, living stones glitter in his callused hands.

"This ring, so old, belonged to my mother; look carefully at the miniature in the other room and you'll see her wearing it. Cousin Begoña would mutter behind her back that a sweetheart of hers . . . "

The ladies in the portraits would move their lips and speak, once again, would breathe again—all these ladies he had seen, he had touched. I would picture them in my mind and understand the meaning of these jewels.

"Have I told you about the time we traveled to Europe, in 1908, before the Revolution? You had to take a ship to Colima. And in Venice your aunt Panchita fell in love with a certain pair of earrings. They were much too expensive, and I told her so. 'They are fit for a queen.' Next day I bought them for her. You just can't imagine what it was like because all this took place long, long before you were born, in 1908, in Venice, when your aunt was so young, so . . . "

"Uncle, you're getting tired, you should rest."

"You're right, I'm tired. Leave me a while and take the small chest to your room. It's yours."

"But, uncle . . . "

"It's all yours, that's all! I trust I can give away whatever I want!"

His voice broke into a sob: the illusion was vanishing and he found himself again on the point of dying, of saying goodbye to the things he had loved. He turned to the wall and I left with the box in my hands, not knowing what to do.

On other occasions he would tell me about "the year of the famine," or "the year of the yellow corn," or "the year of the plague," and very old tales of murderers and ghosts. Once he even tried to sing a *corrido* from his youth, but it shattered in his jagged voice. He was leaving me his life, and he was happy.

The doctor said that yes, he could see some recovery, but that we were not to raise our hopes, there was no cure, it was merely a matter of a few days more or less.

One afternoon of menacing dark clouds, when I was bringing in the clothes hanging out to dry in the courtyard, I heard María cry out. I stood still, listening to her cry as if it were a peal of thunder, the first of the storm to come. Then silence, and I was left alone in the courtyard, motionless. A bee buzzed by and the rain did not fall. No one knows as well as I do how awful a foreboding can be, a premonition hanging above a head turned towards the sky.

"Lichita, he's dying! He's gasping for air!"

"Go get the doctor . . . No! I'll go. But call Doña Clara to stay with you till I'm back."

"And the priest, fetch the priest."

I ran, I ran away from that unbearable moment, blunt and asphyxiating. I ran, hurried back, entered the house, made coffee; I greeted the relatives who began to arrive dressed in half-mourning; I ordered candles; I asked for a few holy relics; I kept on feverishly trying to fulfill my only obligation at the time, to be with my uncle. I asked the doctor: he had given him an injection, so as not to leave anything untried, but he knew it was useless. I saw the priest arrive with the Eucharist, even then I lacked the courage to enter. I knew I would regret it after-wards. "Thank God, now I won't die alone"—but I couldn't. I covered my face with my hands and prayed.

The priest came and touched my shoulder. I thought that all was over and I shivered.

"He's calling you. Come in."

I don't know how I reached the door. Night had fallen and the room, lit by a bedside lamp, seemed enormous. The furniture, larger than life, looked black, and a strange clogging atmosphere hung about the bed. Trembling, I felt I was inhaling death.

"Stand next to him," said the priest.

I obeyed, moving towards the foot of the bed, unable to look even at the sheets.

"Your uncle's wish, unless you say otherwise, is to marry you *in articulo mortis*, so that you may inherit his possessions. Do you accept?"

I stifled a cry of horror. I opened my eyes wide enough to let in the whole terrible room. "Why does he want to drag me into his grave?" I felt death touching my skin.

"Luisa . . . "

It was uncle Apolonio. Now I had to look at him. He could barely mouth the words, his jaw seemed slack and he spoke moving his face like that of a ventriloquist's doll.

"Please."

And he fell silent with exhaustion.

I could take no more. I left the room. That was not my uncle, it did not even look like him. Leave everything to me, yes, but not only his possessions, his stories, his life. I didn't want it, his life, his death. I didn't want it. When I opened my eyes I was standing once again in the courtyard and the sky was still overcast. I breathed in deeply, painfully.

"Already?" the relatives drew near to ask, seeing me so distraught.

I shook my head. Behind me, the priest explained.

"Don Apolonio wants to marry her with his last breath, so that she may inherit him."

"And you won't?" the old servant asked anxiously. "Don't

be silly, no one deserves it more than you. You were a daughter to them, and you have worked very hard looking after him. If you don't marry him, the cousins in Mexico City will leave you without a cent. Don't be silly!"

"It's a fine gesture on his part."

"And afterwards you'll be left a rich widow, as untouched as you are now." A young cousin laughed nervously.

"It's a considerable fortune, and I, as your uncle several times removed, would advise you to . . . "

"If you think about it, not accepting shows a lack of both charity and humility."

"That's true, that's absolutely true."

I did not want to give an old man his last pleasure, a pleasure I should, after all, be thankful for, because my youthful body, of which I felt so proud, had not dwelt in any of the regions of death. I was overcome by nausea. That was my last clear thought that night. I woke from a kind of hypnotic slumber as they forced me to hold his hand covered in cold sweat. I felt nauseous again, but said "yes."

I remember vaguely that they hovered over me all the time, talking all at once, taking me over there, bringing me over here, making me sign, making me answer. The taste of that night —a taste that has stayed with me for the rest of my life—was that of an evil ring-around-the-rosies turning vertiginously around me, while everyone laughed and sang grotesquely

> *This is the way the widow is wed,*
> *The widow is wed, the widow is wed*

while I stood, a slave, in the middle. Something inside me hurt, and I could not lift my eyes.

When I came to my senses, all was over, and on my hand

shone the braided ring which I had seen so many times on my aunt Panchita's finger: there had been no time for anything else.

The guests began to leave.

"If you need me, don't hesitate to call. In the meantime give him these drops every six hours."

"May God bless you and give you strength."

"Happy honeymoon," whispered the young cousin in my ear, with a nasty laugh.

I returned to the sickbed. "Nothing has changed, nothing has changed." My fear certainly had not changed. I convinced María to stay and help me look after uncle Apolonio. I only calmed down once I saw dawn was breaking. It had started to rain, but without thunder or lightning, very still.

It kept on drizzling that day and the next, and the day after. Four days of anguish. Nobody came to visit, nobody other than the doctor and the priest. On days like these no one goes out, everyone stays indoors and waits for life to start again. These are the days of the spirit, sacred days.

If at least the sick man had needed plenty of attention my hours would have seemed shorter, but there was little that could be done for him.

On the fourth night María went to bed in a room close by, and I stayed alone with the dying man. I was listening to the monotonous rain and praying unconsciously, half asleep and unafraid, waiting. My fingers stopped turning the rosary, and as I held the beads I could feel through my fingertips a peculiar warmth, a warmth both alien and intimate, the warmth we leave in things and which is returned to us transformed, a comrade, a brother foreshadowing the warmth of others, a warmth both unknown and recollected, never quite grasped and yet inhabiting the core of my bones. Softly, deliciously, my nerves relaxed, my fingers felt light, I fell asleep.

I must have slept many hours: it was dawn when I woke up. I knew because the lights had been switched off and the electric plant stops working at two in the morning. The room, barely lit by an oil lamp at the feet of the Holy Virgin on the chest of drawers, made me think of the wedding night, *my* wedding night. It was so long ago, an empty eternity.

From the depth of the gloomy darkness don Apolonio's broken and tired breathing reached me. There he still was, not the man himself, simply the persistent and incomprehensible shred that hangs on, with no goal, with no apparent motive. Death is frightening, but life mingled with death, soaked in death, is horrible in a way that owes little to either life or death. Silence, corruption of the flesh, the stench, the monstrous transformation, the final vanishing act, all this is painful, but it reaches a climax and then gives way, dissolves into the earth, into memory, into history. But not this: this arrangement worked out between life and death—echoed in the useless exhaling and inhaling—could carry on forever. I would hear him trying to clear his anaesthetized throat and it occurred to me that air was not entering that body, or rather, that it was not a human body breathing the air: it was a machine, puffing and panting, stopping in a curious game, a game to kill time without end. That thing was no human being: it was somebody playing with huffs and snores. And the horror of it all won me over: I began to breathe to the rhythm of his panting; to inhale, stop suddenly, choke, breathe, choke again, unable to control myself, until I realized I had been deceived by what I thought was the sense of the game. What I really felt was the pain and shortness of breath of an animal in pain. But I kept on, on, until there was one single breathing, one single inhuman breath, one single agony. I felt calmer, terrified but calmer: I had lifted the barrier, I could let myself go and simply wait for the common end.

It seemed to me that by abandoning myself, by giving myself up unconditionally, the end would happen quickly, would not be allowed to continue. It would have fulfilled its purpose and its persistent search in the world.

Not a hint of farewell, not a glimmer of pity towards me. I carried on the mortal game for a long, long while, from someplace where time had ceased to matter.

The shared breathing became less agitated, more peaceful, but also weaker. I seemed to be drifting back. I felt so tired I could barely move, exhaustion nestling in forever inside my body. I opened my eyes. Nothing had changed.

No: far away, in the shadows, is a rose. Alone, unique, alive. There it is, cut out against the darkness, clear as day, with its fleshy, luminous petals, shining. I look at it and my hand moves and I remember its touch and the simple act of putting it in a vase. I looked at it then, but I only understand it now. I stir, I blink, and the rose is still there, in full bloom, identical to itself.

I breathe freely, with my own breath. I pray, I remember, I doze off, and the untouched rose mounts guard over the dawning light and my secret. Death and hope suffer change.

And now day begins to break and in the clean sky I see that at last the days of rain are over. I stay at the window a long time, watching everything change in the sun. A strong ray enters and the suffering seems a lie. Unjustified bliss fills my lungs and unwittingly I smile. I turn to the rose as if to an accomplice but I can't find it: the sun has withered it.

Clear days came again, and maddening heat. The people went to work, and sang, but don Apolonio would not die; in fact he seemed to get better. I kept on looking after him, but no longer in a cheerful mood—my eyes downcast, I turned the guilt I felt into hard work. My wish, now clearly, was that it all end, that he die. The fear, the horror I felt looking at him, at his touch, his voice, were unjustified because the link between us was not real, could never be real, and yet he felt like a dead weight upon me. Through politeness and shame I wanted to get rid of it.

Yes, don Apolonio was visibly improving. Even the doctor was surprised and offered no explanation.

On the very first morning I sat him up among the pillows, I noticed that certain look in my uncle's eyes. The heat was stifling and I had to lift him all by myself. Once I had propped him up I noticed: the old man was staring as if dazed at my heaving chest, his face distorted and his trembling hands unconsciously moving towards me. I drew back instinctively and turned my head away.

"Please close the blinds, it's too hot."

His almost dead body was growing warm.

"Come here, Luisa, sit by my side. Come."

"Yes, uncle." I sat, my knees drawn up, at the foot of the bed, without looking at him.

"Polo, you must call me Polo, after all we are closer relatives now." There was mockery in the tone of his voice.

"Yes, uncle."

"Polo, Polo." His voice was again sweet and soft. "You'll have a lot to forgive me. I'm old and sick, and a man in my condition is like a child."

"Yes."

"Let's see. Try saying, 'Yes, Polo.' "

"Yes, Polo."

The name on my lips seemed to me an aberration, made me nauseated.

Polo got better, but became fussy and irritable. I realized he was fighting to be the man he once had been, and yet the resurrected self was not the same, but another.

"Luisa, bring me . . . Luisa, give me . . . Luisa, plump up my pillows . . . pour me some water . . . prop up my leg . . . "

He wanted me to be there all day long, always by his side, seeing to his needs, touching him. And the fixed look and distorted face kept coming back, more and more frequently, growing over his features like a mask.

"Pick up my book. It fell underneath the bed, on this side."

I kneeled and stuck my head and almost half my body underneath the bed, and had to stretch my arm as far as it would go, to reach it. At first I thought it had been my own movements, or maybe the bedclothes, but once I had the book in my hand and was shuffling to get out, I froze, stunned by what I had long foreseen, even expected: the outburst, the scream, the thunder. A rage never before felt raced through me when the realization of what was happening reached my consciousness, when his shaking hand, taking advantage of my amazement, became surer and heavier, and enjoyed itself, adventuring with no restraints, feeling and exploring my thighs—a fleshless hand glued to my skin, fingering my body with delight, a dead hand searching impatiently between my legs, a bodyless hand.

I rose as quickly as I could, my face burning with shame and determination, but when I saw him I forgot myself and entered like an automaton into the nightmare. Polo was laughing softly through his toothless mouth. And then, suddenly serious, with a coolness that terrified me, he said:

"What? Aren't you my wife before God and men? Come here, I'm cold, heat my bed. But first take off your dress, you don't want to get it creased."

What followed, I know, is my story, my life, but I can barely remember it; like a disgusting dream I can't even tell whether it was long or short. Only one thought kept me sane during the early days: "This can't go on, it can't go on." I imagined that God would not allow it, would prevent it in some way or another. He, personally, God, would interfere. Death, once dreaded, seemed my only hope. Not Apolonio's—he was a demon of death—but mine, the just and necessary death for my corrupted flesh. But nothing happened. Everything stayed on, suspended in time, without future. Then, one morning, taking nothing with me, I left.

It was useless. Three days later they let me know that my husband was dying, and they called me back. I went to see the father confessor and told him my story.

"What keeps him alive is lust, the most horrible of all sins. This isn't life, Father, it's death. Let him die!"

"He would die in despair. I can't allow it."

"And I?"

"I understand, but if you don't go to him, it would be like murder. Try not to arouse him, pray to the Blessed Virgin, and keep your mind on your duties."

I went back. And lust drew him out of the grave once more.

Fighting, endlessly fighting, I managed, after several years, to overcome my hatred, and finally, at the very end, I even conquered the beast: Apolonio died in peace, sweetly, his old self again.

But I was not able to go back to who I was. Now wickedness, malice, shine in the eyes of the men who look at me, and I feel I have become an occasion of sin for all, I, the vilest of harlots. Alone, a sinner, totally engulfed by the never-ending flames of this cruel summer which surrounds us all, like an army of ants.

Translated by Alberto Manguel

THE SHUNAMMITE

Cooking Lesson

Rosario Castellanos

The kitchen is shining white. It's a shame to have to get it dirty. One ought to sit down and contemplate it, describe it, close one's eyes, evoke it. Looking closely, this spotlessness, this pulchritude lacks the glaring excess that causes chills in hospitals. Or is it the halo of disinfectants, the rubber-cushioned steps of the aides, the hidden presence of sickness and death? What do I care? My place is here. I've been here from the beginning of time. In the German proverb, woman is synonymous with *Küche, Kinder, Kirche*. I wandered astray through classrooms, streets, offices, cafés, wasting my time on skills that now I must forget in order to acquire others. For example, choosing the menu. How could one carry out such an arduous task without the cooperation of society—of all history? On a special shelf, just right for my height, my guardian spirits are lined up, those acclaimed jugglers that reconcile the most irreducible contradictions among the pages of their recipe books: slimness and gluttony, pleasing appearance and economy, speed and succulence. With their infinite combinations: slimness and economy, speed and pleasing appearance, succulence and . . . What can you suggest to me for today's meal, O experienced housewife, inspiration of mothers here and gone, voice of tradition, clamoring secret of the supermarkets? I open a book at random and read: "Don Quixote's Dinner." Very literary but not very satisfying, because Don Quixote was not famous as a gourmet but as a bumbler. Although a more profound analysis of the text reveals etc., etc., etc. Ugh! More ink has flowed about that character than water under bridges. "Fowl Center-Face." Esoteric. Whose face? Does the face of someone or something have a center? If it does, it must not be very appetizing. "Bigos Roumanian." Well, just who do you think you're talking to? If I knew what tarragon or *ananas* were I wouldn't be consulting this book, because I'd know a lot of other things, too. If you had the slightest sense of reality, you yourself or any of your colleagues would take the trouble to write a dictionary of technical terms, edit a few prolegomena, invent a propaedeutic to make the difficult culinary art accessible to the lay person. But you all start from the assumption that we're all in on the secret and you limit yourselves to stating it. I, at least, solemnly declare that I am not, and never have been, in on either this or any other secret you share. I never understood anything about anything. You observe the symptoms: I stand here like an imbecile, in an impeccable and neutral kitchen, wearing the apron that I usurp in order to give a pretense of efficiency and of which I will be shamefully but justly stripped.

I open the refrigerator drawer that proclaims "Meat" and extract a package that I cannot recognize under its icy coating. I thaw it in hot water, revealing the title without which I never would have identified the contents: Fancy Beef Broil. Wonderful. A plain and wholesome dish. But since it doesn't mean resolving an antinomy or proposing an axiom, it doesn't appeal to me.

Moreover, it's not simply an excess of logic that inhibits my hunger. It's also the appearance of it, frozen stiff; it's the color that shows now that I've ripped open the package. Red, as if it were just about to start bleeding.

Our backs were that same color, my husband and I, after our orgiastic sunbathing on the beaches of Acapulco. He could afford the luxury of "behaving like the man he is" and stretch out face down to avoid rubbing his painful skin. But I, self-sacrificing little Mexican wife, born like a dove to the nest, smiled like Cuauhtémoc under torture on the rack when he said, "My bed is not made of roses," and fell silent. Face up, I bore not only my own weight but also his on top of me. The classic position for making love. And I moaned, from the tearing and the pleasure. The classic moan. Myths, myths.

The best part (for my sunburn at least) was when he fell asleep. Under my fingertips—not very sensitive due to prolonged contact with typewriter keys—the nylon of my bridal nightgown slipped away in a fraudulent attempt to look like lace. I played with the tips of the buttons and those other ornaments that make whoever wears them seem so feminine in the late night darkness. The whiteness of my clothes, deliberate, repetitive, immodestly symbolic, was temporarily abolished. Perhaps at some moment it managed to accomplish its purpose beneath the light and the glance of those eyes that are now overcome by fatigue.

Eyelids close and behold, once again, exile. An enormous sandy expanse with no juncture other than the sea, whose movement suggests paralysis, with no invitation except that of the cliff to suicide.

But that's a lie. I'm not the dream that dreams in a dream that dreams; I'm not the reflection of an image in a glass; I'm not annihilated by the closing off of a consciousness or of all possible consciousness. I go on living a dense, viscose, turbid life even though the man at my side and the one far away ignore me, forget me, postpone me, abandon me, fall out of love with me.

COOKING LESSON

I too am a consciousness that can close itself off, abandon someone, and expose him to annihilation. I . . . The meat, under the sprinkling of salt, has toned down some of its offensive redness and now it seems more tolerable, more familiar to me. It's that piece I saw a thousand times without realizing it, when I used to pop in to tell the cook that . . .

We weren't born together. Our meeting was due to accident. A happy one? It's still too soon to say. We met by chance at an exhibition, a lecture, a film. We ran into each other in the elevator; he gave me his seat on the tram; a guard interrupted our perplexed and parallel contemplation of the giraffe because it was time to close the zoo. Someone, he or I, it's all the same, asked the stupid but indispensable question: Do you work or study? A harmony of interests and of good intentions, a show of "serious" intentions. A year ago I hadn't the slightest idea of his existence and now I'm lying close to him with our thighs entwined, damp with sweat and semen. I could get up without waking him, walk barefoot to the shower. To purify myself? I feel no revulsion. I prefer to believe that what links him to me is something as easy to wipe away as a secretion and not as terrible as a sacrament.

So I remain still, breathing rhythmically to imitate drowsiness, my insomnia the only spinster's jewel I've kept and I'm inclined to keep until death.

Beneath the brief deluge of pepper the meat seems to have gone gray. I banish this sign of aging by rubbing it as though I were trying to penetrate the surface and impregnate its thickness with flavors, because I lost my old name and I still can't get used to the new one, which is not mine either. When some employee pages me in the lobby of the hotel I remain deaf with thin vague uneasiness that is the prelude to recognition. Who could that person be who doesn't answer? It could be something urgent, serious, a matter of life or death. The caller goes away without leaving a clue, a message, or even the possibility of another meeting. Is it anxiety that presses against my heart? No, it's his hand pressing on my shoulder and his lips smiling at me in benevolent mockery, more like a sorcerer than a master.

So then, I accept, as we head toward the bar (my peeling shoulder feels like it's on fire), that it's true that in my contact or collision with him I've undergone a profound metamorphosis. I didn't know and now I know; I didn't feel and now I do feel; I wasn't and now I am.

It should be left to sit for a while. Until it reaches room temperature, until it's steeped in the flavors that I've rubbed into it. I have the feeling I didn't know how to calculate very well and that I've bought a piece that's too big for the two of us—for me, because I'm lazy, not a carnivore; for him, for aesthetic reasons because he's watching his waistline. Almost all of it will be left over! Yes, I already know that I shouldn't worry: one of the good fairies that hovers over me is going to come to my rescue and explain how one uses leftovers. It's a mistake, anyhow. You don't start married life in such a sordid way. I'm afraid that you also don't start it with a dish as dull as broiled beef.

Thanks, I murmur, while I wipe my lips with a corner of the napkin. Thanks for the transparent cocktail glass, and for the submerged olive. Thanks for letting me out of the cage of one sterile routine only to lock me into the cage of another, a routine which according to all purposes and possibilities must be fruitful. Thanks for giving me the chance to show off a long gown with a train, for helping me walk up the aisle of the church, carried away by the organ music. Thanks for . . .

How long will it take to be done? Well, that shouldn't worry me too much because it has to be put on the grill at the last minute. It takes very little time, according to the cookbook. How long is little? Fifteen minutes? Ten? Five? Naturally the text doesn't specify, it presupposes an intuition which, according to my sex, I'm supposed to possess but I don't, a sense I was born without that would allow me to gauge the precise minute the meat is done.

And what about you? Don't you have anything to thank me for? You've specified it with a slightly pedantic solemnity and a precision that perhaps were meant to flatter but instead offended: my virginity. When you discovered it I felt like the last dinosaur on a planet where the species was extinct. I longed to justify myself, to explain that if I was intact when I met you it was not out of virtue or pride or ugliness but simply out of adherence to a style. I'm not baroque. The tiny imperfection in the pearl is unbearable to me. The only alternative I have is the neoclassic one, and its rigidity is incompatible with the spontaneity needed for making love. I lack that ease of the person who rows or plays tennis or dances. I don't play any sports. I comply with the ritual but my move to surrender petrifies into a statue.

Are you monitoring my transit to fluidity? Do you expect it, do you need it? Or is this hieraticism that sanctifies you, and that you interpret as the passivity natural to my nature, enough for you? So if you are voluble it will ease your mind to think that I won't hinder your adventures. It won't be necessary—thanks to my temperament—for you to fatten me up, tie me down hand and foot with children, gag me on the thick honey of resignation. I'll stay the same as I am. Calm. When you throw your body on top of mine I feel as though a gravestone were covering me, full of inscriptions, strange names, memorable dates. You moan unintelligibly and I'd like to whisper my name in your ear to remind you who it is you are possessing.

I'm myself. But who am I? Your wife, of course. And that title suffices to distinguish me from past memories or future projects. I bear an owner's brand, a property tag, and yet you watch me suspiciously. I'm not weaving a web to trap you. I'm not a praying mantis. I appreciate your believing such a hypothesis, but it's false.

This meat has a toughness and a consistency that is not like beef. It must be mammoth. One of those that have been preserved since prehistoric times in the Siberian ice, that the peasants thaw out and fix for food. In that terribly boring documentary they showed at the embassy, so full of superfluous details, there wasn't the slightest mention of how long it took to make them edible. Years, months? And I only have so much time.

Is that a lark? Or is it a nightingale? No, our schedule won't be ruled by such winged creatures as those that announced the coming of dawn to Romeo and Juliet but by a noisy and unerring alarm clock. And you will not descend today by the stairway of my tresses but rather on the steps of detailed complaints: you've lost a button off your jacket; the toast is burned; the coffee is cold.

I'll ruminate my resentment in silence. All the responsibilities and duties of a servant are assigned to me for everything. I'm supposed to keep the house impeccable, the clothes ready, mealtimes exact. But I'm not paid any salary; I don't get one day a week off; I can't change masters. On the other hand, I'm supposed to contribute to the support of the household and I'm expected to efficiently carry out a job where the boss is demanding, my colleagues conspire, and my subordinates hate me. In my free time I transform myself into a society matron who gives luncheons and dinners for her husband's friends, attends meetings, subscribes to the opera season, watches her weight, renews her wardrobe, cares for her skin, keeps herself attractive, keeps up on all the gossip, stays up late and gets up early, runs the monthly risk of maternity, has no suspicions about the evening executive meetings, the business trips and the arrival of unexpected clients; who suffers from olfactory hallucinations when she catches a whiff of French perfume (different from the one she uses) on her husband's shirts and handkerchiefs and on lonely nights refuses to think why or what so much fuss is all about and fixes herself a stiff drink and reads a detective story with the fragile mood of a convalescent.

Shouldn't it be time to turn on the stove? Low flame so the broiler will start warming up gradually, "which should be greased first so the meat will not stick." That did occur to me; there was no need to waste pages on those recommendations.

I'm very awkward. Now it's called awkwardness, but it used to be called innocence and you loved it. But I've never loved it. When I was single I used to read things on the sly, perspiring from the arousal and shame. I never found out anything. My breasts ached, my eyes got misty, my muscles contracted in a spasm of nausea.

The oil is starting to get hot. I let it get too hot, heavy handed that I am, and now it's spitting and spattering and burning me. That's how I'm going to fry in those narrow hells, through my fault, through my fault, through my most grievous fault. But child, you're not the only one. All your classmates do the same thing or worse. They confess in the confessional, do their penance, are forgiven and fall into it again. All of them. If I had continued going around with them they'd be questioning me now, the married ones to find things out for themselves, the single ones to find out how far they can go. Impossible to let them down. I would invent acrobatics, sublime fainting spells, transports as they're called in the *Thousand and One Nights*

—records! If you only heard me then, you'd never recognize me, Casanova!

I drop the meat onto the grill and instinctively step back against the wall. What a noise! Now it's stopped. The meat lies there silently, faithful to its deceased state. I still think it's too big.

It's not that you've let me down. It's true that I didn't expect anything special. Gradually we'll reveal ourselves to one another, discover our secrets, our little tricks, learn to please each other. And one day you and I will become a pair of perfect lovers and then, right in the middle of an embrace, we'll disappear and the words, "The End," will appear on the screen.

What's the matter? The meat is shrinking. No, I'm not seeing things; I'm not wrong. You can see the mark of its original size by the outline that it left on the grill. It was only a little bit bigger. Good! Maybe it will be just the right size for our appetites.

In my next movie I'd like them to give me a different part. The white sorceress in a savage village? No, today I don't feel much inclined to either heroism or danger. Better a famous woman (a fashion designer or something like that), rich and independent, who lives by herself in an apartment in New York, Paris, or London. Her occasional *affaires* entertain her but do not change her. She's not sentimental. After a breakup scene she lights a cigarette and surveys the urban scenery through the picture window of her studio.

Ah, the color of the meat looks much better now, only raw in a few obstinate places. But the rest is browned and gives off a delicious aroma. Will it be enough for the two of us? It looks very small to me.

If I got dressed up now I'd try on one of those dresses from my trousseau and go out. What would happen, hmmmm? Maybe an older man with a car would pick me up. Mature. Retired. The only kind who can afford to be on the make at this time of day.

What the devil's going on? This damned meat is starting to give off horrible black smoke! I should have turned it over! Burned on one side. Well, thank goodness it has another one.

Miss, if you will allow me . . . Mrs.! And I'm warning you, my husband is very jealous . . . Then he shouldn't let you go out alone. You're a temptation to any passerby. Nobody in this world says passerby. Pedestrian? Only the newspapers when they report accidents. You're a temptation for anyone. Mean-ing-ful silence. The glances of a sphinx. The older man is following me at a safe distance. Better for him. Better for me, because on the corner—uh, oh—my husband, who's spying on me and who never leaves me alone morning, noon, or night, who suspects everything and everybody. Your Honor, it's impossible to live this way, I want a divorce.

Now what? This piece of meat's mother never told it that it was meat and ought to act like it. It's curling up like a corkscrew pastry. Anyhow, I don't know where all that smoke can be coming from if I turned the stove off ages ago. Of course, Dear Abby, what one must do now is open the window, plug in the ventilator so it won't be smelly when my husband gets here. And I'll so cutely run right out to greet him at the door with my best dress on, my best smile, and my warmest invitation to eat out.

It's a thought. We'll look at the restaurant menu while that miserable piece of charred meat lies hidden at the bottom of the garbage pail. I'll be careful not to mention the incident because I'd be considered a somewhat irresponsible wife, with frivolous tendencies but not mentally retarded. This is the

ROSARIO CASTELLANOS

initial public image that I project and I've got to maintain it even though it isn't accurate.

There's another possibility. Don't open the window, don't turn on the ventilator, don't throw the meat in the garbage. When my husband gets here let him smell it like the ogres in all the stories and tell him that no, it doesn't smell of human flesh here, but of useless woman. I'll exaggerate my compunction so he can be magnanimous. After all, what's happened is so normal! What newlywed doesn't do the same thing that I've done? When we visit my mother-in-law, who is still at the stage of not attacking me because she doesn't know my weak points yet, she'll tell me her own experiences. The time, for example, when her husband asked her to fix coddled eggs and she took him literally . . . ha, ha. Did that stop her from becoming a fabulous widow, I mean a fabulous cook? Because she was widowed much later and for other reasons. After that she gave free rein to her maternal instincts and spoiled everything with all her pampering.

No, he's not going to find it the least bit amusing. He's going to say that I got distracted, that it's the height of carelessness and, yes, condescendingly, I'm going to accept his accusations.

But it isn't true, it isn't. I was watching the meat all the time, watching how a series of very odd things happened to it. Saint Theresa was right when she said that God is in the stewpots. Or matter is energy or whatever it's called now.

Let's backtrack. First there's the piece of meat, one color, one shape, one size. Then it changes, looks even nicer and you feel very happy. Then it starts changing again and now it doesn't look so nice. It keeps changing and changing and changing and you just can't tell when you should stop it. Because if I leave this piece of meat on the grill indefinitely, it will burn to a crisp till nothing is left of it. So that piece of meat that gave the impression of being so solid and real no longer exists.

So? My husband also gives the impression of being solid and real when we're together, when I touch him, when I see him. He certainly changes and I change too, although so slowly that neither of us realizes it. Then he goes off and suddenly becomes a memory and . . . Oh, no, I'm not going to fall into that trap; the one about the invented character and the invented narrator and the invented anecdote. Besides, it's not the consequence that licitly follows from the meat episode.

The meat hasn't stopped existing. It has undergone a series of metamorphoses. And the fact that it ceases to be perceptible for the senses does not mean that the cycle is concluded but that it has taken the quantum leap. It will go on operating on other levels. On the level of my consciousness, my memory, my will, changing me, defining me, establishing the course of my future.

From today on, I'll be whatever I choose to be at the moment. Seductively unbalanced, deeply withdrawn, hypocritical. From the very beginning I will impose, just a bit insolently, the rules of the game. My husband will resent the appearance of my dominance, which will widen like the ripples on the surface of the water when someone has skipped a pebble across it. I'll struggle to prevail and, if he gives in, I'll retaliate with my scorn, and, if he doesn't give in, I'll simply be unable to forgive him.

If I assume another attitude, if I'm the typical case, femininity that begs indulgence for her errors, the balance will tip in favor of my antagonist and I will be running the race with a handicap, which, apparently, seals my defeat, and which, essentially, guarantees my triumph by the winding path that my grandmothers took, the humble ones, the ones who didn't open their mouths except to say yes and achieved an obedience foreign to even their most irrational whims. The recipe of course is ancient and its efficiency is proven. If I still doubt, all I have to do is ask my neighbor. She'll confirm my certainty.

It's just that it revolts me to behave that way. This definition is not applicable to me, the former one either; neither corresponds to my inner truth, nor safeguards my authenticity. Must I grasp one of them and bind myself to its terms only because it is a cliché accepted by the majority and intelligible to everyone? And it's not because I'm a *rara avis*. You can say about me what Pfandl said about Sor Juana, that I belong to the class of hesitant neurotics. The diagnosis is very easy, but what consequences does the assumption hold?

If I insist on affirming my version of the facts my husband is going to look at me suspiciously; he's going to live in continual expectation that I'll be declared insane.

Our life together could not be more problematic! He doesn't want conflicts of any kind, much less such abstract, absurd, metaphysical conflicts as the one I would present him with. His home is a haven of peace where he takes refuge from all the storms of life. Agreed. I accepted that when I got married and I was even ready to accept sacrifice for the sake of marital harmony. But I counted on the fact that the sacrifice, the complete renunciation of what I am, would only be demanded of me on The Sublime Occasion, at The Time of Heroic Solutions, at The Moment of the Definitive Decision. Not in exchange for what I stumbled on today, which is something very insignificant and very ridiculous. And yet . . .

Translated by Maureen Ahern

COOKING LESSON

Tachas

Efrén Hernández

It was thirty-five minutes past six in the afternoon.

The teacher said, "What, then, are *tachas*?" But my thoughts were elsewhere; besides, I'd come to class unprepared that day.

In the room where these events took place, there are three wooden doors painted red, and set into each panel there's glass, frosted on the bottom half.

From where I was sitting, you could see through the un-frosted section of glass in the door at the head of the class-room: a piece of wall, part of a door, and some electrical wires from the lighting fixture installation. Through the door at mid-classroom, the same could be seen. Exactly the same, more or less. And finally, through the third door, the molding on the capital of a column, plus a tiny, triangular patch of sky.

Clouds. Slowly, clouds would pass by across this small tri-angle. The entire time I hadn't seen anything go by but clouds, except a quick, agile, fleeting bird.

It's very entertaining, contemplating clouds. Clouds that pass by, clouds that change shape, spreading out, stretching, twisting, breaking up against the blue sky just after the rain has ended.

The teacher said:

"What, then, are *tachas*?"

The odd little word crept inside my ears like a mouse in its hole, and stayed there, crouching. Afterwards came silence, on tiptoe. A silence that, like all silences, made no sound.

I'm not sure why, but I surmise that what brought me back to the real world, even if it was only halfway, weren't the words themselves, but the silence that ensued, because the teacher had been talking for quite some time, and yet, I'd heard nothing.

"*Tachas*? But, what in the world are *tachas*?" I thought. "Who knows what in the world *tachas* are? No one even knows what in the world the world is. No one knows anything, anything at all."

As for me, to use myself as an example, I can't say what I am, or even what I'm doing here, much less why I'm doing it. I don't know if it's right or wrong, either. Because who can tell for sure whether he's happened upon his true path? Who can say for certain that he hasn't made a mistake?

There will always be this primordial doubt.

Along life's paths, numerous crossroads appear. Which ones will our steps lead us down? Out of those twenty, those thirty, those thousand paths, which will be the one that, once taken, won't make us wonder if we haven't erred?

Now the sky was covered with clouds once again. They were growing thicker and thicker; there was only a tiny spot of blue left, the size of a nickel. A light, steady rain was falling. Mathematically vertical, because the air was as still as a statue.

In the book *The Labors of Persiles and Sigismunda*, Cervantes portrays motionless plains. And on them, pilgrims under a gray sky. And on their minds, this same problem. Not once during the entire book does he manage to come up with an answer.

This problem doesn't bother animals, or plants, or stones. They've come up with a simple solution: bowing to Nature's will. Water does what it's supposed to perfectly well, running downhill, never attempting to go up.

EFRÉN HERNÁNDEZ

In fact, it would seem that Cervantes did solve it. Not through Persiles, though, who was sane, but through the madman Don Quixote.

Don Quixote loosed his horse's reins, and felt safer and more secure than we do.

The teacher said:

"What, then, are *tachas*?"

Under the arch, on the wire perched a small, earth-colored bird, ruffling its feathers to shake off the rain.

The bird sang, oooo, phee pheeee, phee pheeee. This was clearly a very contented little bird. He sang in the air with his throat opened wide, but once he'd sung, he became pensive. No doubt he was thinking, no, this song isn't elegant enough. But that was all wrong. I grasped, or thought I grasped, that the bird wasn't thinking sincere thoughts. The truth lay elsewhere. Actually it was the maid whistling that song, and he felt a certain aversion towards her, because when she cleaned his cage, she did so begrudgingly and in haste.

The maid in that house, was her name Imelda? No. Imelda is a girl who sells Elegant cigarettes, Monarch cigarettes, chocolates, and matches down at the corner store. Margarita? No, her name isn't Margarita, either. Margarita's a name for a young, pretty woman with long, white hands and golden eyes. Petra? Yes, now that's a maid's name. Or Tacha, maybe.

What in the world was I thinking, when I said no one knows what a *tacha* is?

What a shame that the bird's gone now. Which way has the little bird gone? He's probably perched on some other wire, singing oooo pheeeee, but I can't hear him anymore. Such a shame.

The sky was clearing a bit already, the rain had let up for awhile. Dusk was falling slowly. The rising shadows brought deeper meaning into the sky. The same as every other night, the same stars as always, began to shine in order of distance and stature.

From below, the noise of an entire city rose; from above, the silence of all infinity fell.

In fact, I don't know what it is about the sky here that reveals the universe through a veil of sadness.

There, afternoons like this one are very rare. They nearly always boast a transparent sky, dyed a marvelous blue, like none I've ever found anywhere else. Once the night starts to fall, you can see stars in its depths, countless stars. Like tiny, golden grains of sand beneath waters that have the privilege of being crystal clear.

There, the moon's features can be seen more clearly than anywhere else. Whoever hasn't been there, doesn't really know what the moon can be. Maybe that's why people around here sustain the idea that the moon is melancholy. Now that's one of the great lies of literature. As if the moon could be melancholy!

The moon is smiling, blushing. But the thing is, around here, they don't know her. Her smile is soft, and behind her lips, tiny, fine teeth show like pearls, and her eyes are violet, that lilac-tinged color we see at the break of day, and around the rings under her eyes, small bunches of violets flourish, like they are wont to do around deep springs.

There, everything is immaculate, there, everything is free of *tachas* . . . *tachas*, again, *tachas*. What in the world was I thinking, when I said no one knows what *tachas* are?

All this I'd been thinking at the typical speed of thought, and God only knows what I would have gone on thinking, if the teacher hadn't repeated for the fourth or fifth time, but in a louder voice now:

EFRÉN HERNÁNDEZ

"What, then, are *tachas*?"

And he added:

"I'm asking you, Mr Juárez."

"Me, teacher?"

"Yes. You, sir."

That's when many things hit me. In the first place, everyone was staring at me. Second, there could be no doubt that the teacher was addressing me. Third, the teacher's beard and moustache looked like clouds in the shape of a beard and a moustache. And fourth, well, there were a few other things. But the truly serious matter at hand was the second.

And then I was assailed with that devious standby of all bad students, bad advice, which assured me it was absolutely necessary to say something.

"The worst thing you can do is say nothing," they'd told me. And so, half-awake still, I said the first thing without rhyme or reason that came into my head.

I wouldn't be capable of repeating the sequence my brain, filled with all those birds and clouds, followed in order to muddle through. At any rate, they listened earnestly to everything I came up with.

"Well, teacher, there are many definitions for that word, and given that there's still plenty of time, since we've got another half an hour left, I shall endeavor to examine each and every one of these, starting with the least important, then proceeding according to each item's rank."

Rest assured, I am not insane. If I were, why would I deny it? What's happening here is something else, something not worth explaining, because the explanation is far too lengthy. Thus, on the occasion I'm referring to, it was as if I were talking to myself, monologuing. I can't help but notice, you remain silent.

TACHAS

At the time, you meant nothing to me. According to reality, you should have been the teacher; according to grammar, whoever was being addressed. But to me, you were no one, absolutely no one. You were the imaginary character I speak to whenever I'm alone. If we were to attempt to grant this word its rightful place among the pigeonholes of analogy, it would belong among the pronouns; yet it's not a personal pronoun, or any pronoun that has already been classified. It's a personal pronoun of sorts that can be defined as such, more or less. A word I use sometimes to pretend I'm talking to someone, when actually, I'm alone. I continued:

"I can't help but notice you remain silent, and since silence implies consent, I will proceed in keeping with the manner I've described. The first definition is, therefore, as follows. Third person present indicative of the verb *tachar*, which means: to cross out a word, line, or number that's been miswritten. Now, the second definition is quite different. If a person bears the name Anastasia, whoever holds her in high regard will use this word to designate her. Ergo, her boyfriend will say:

" 'You're life itself to me, Tacha.'

"And her mother:

" 'Tacha, have you swept your father's room yet?'

"And her brother:

" 'Come on, Tacha, sew this button on for me!'

"And finally, to make a long story short, her husband, if he finds her too slovenly (Tacha can fill in for Ramona, here), he will abandon her little by little, without saying anything.

"The third definition forms part of an adverbial phrase and has to do exclusively with one of many ways in which squash can be prepared. Who hasn't heard, at one time or another, the term, *calabaza en tacha*? And finally, there's the meaning construed by our legal code."

And here, I intoned a period, in such a way that it was clear to all.

Orteguita, a patient teacher who lectured us regarding legal proceedings with the magnanimity of a saint, pressed on good-naturedly:

"So tell us, sir, what meaning does it have in the code of law?"

Somewhat inhibited at this point, I came clean:

"Now that's the one definition I don't know. Begging your pardon, teacher, but . . . "

Everybody laughed: Aguilar, Jiménez Tavera, Poncianito, Elodia Cruz, Orteguita. They all laughed, all except for me and *Opossum*, who are not of this world.

I didn't find it humorous, but in theory, it would seem nearly anything that's absurd will make people laugh. Perhaps because we are in a world where everything's absurd, the absurd seems natural and the natural, absurd. And that's the way I am. It seems only natural to me to be what I am. Not to the others, though. To the others, I'm eccentric.

According to Gómez de la Serna,[1] it would be only natural if sleeping birds fell out of trees. And we're all very much aware, no matter how absurd it seems, that birds don't fall.

Now I'm back out on the street. A light rain is falling and, seeing how it rains, I'm certain that far away, lost among the streets, there's someone behind a windowpane, crying because it rains this way.

Translated by Tanya Huntington

---

[1] *Gómez de la Serna*: Spanish writer Ramón Gómez de la Serna (1888-1963), best known for "greguerías"—a short form of poetry that roughly corresponds to the one-liner in comedy.

What Became of Pampa Hash?

JORGE IBARGÜENGOITIA

How did she arrive? Where did she come from? No one knows.
The first indication I had of her presence was the panties.

I had just entered the cabin (the only one) with the intention of opening and eating a can of sardines, when I noticed
a clothesline strung lengthwise above the table, and on it, precisely at the height of the diners' eyes were hanging the panties.
A short while later I heard someone flush the toilet and when
I raised my eyes I saw an image which would later become
more familiar: Pampa Hash coming out of the bathroom. She
looked at me as only a doctor of philosophy could: ignoring
everything, the table, the sardines, the panties, the ocean that
makes us seasick, everything, except my powerful masculinity.

We did not get anywhere that day. Actually, nothing happened. We did not even say hello. She looked at me and I at
her, she went out on deck and I remained inside eating sardines.
One cannot say then, as some viperish tongues have insinuated,
that we have been victims of love at first sight: rather it was the
ennui that brought us together.

Not even our second meeting was definitive from an erotic
viewpoint.

Three men and I were on the bank of the river trying to in-
flate a rubber raft when we saw her appear in her bathing suit.
She was astounding. Possessed by that impulse that makes a

195

man want to marry Mother Earth from time to time, I grabbed the pump and proceeded to pump away like a madman. After five minutes the raft was about to burst and my hands were covered with blisters that later developed into sores. She was looking at me.

"She thinks I'm terrific," I thought in English. We threw the raft into the water and navigated in it as Lord Baden-Powell once said, "on the river of life."

Oh, what a Homeric journey! I broke off pieces of enormous tree trunks with my bare and blistered hands in order to heat the meal and blew on the fire to the point of almost losing consciousness. Later I climbed onto a rock and dived from a height that normally would have given me a cold sweat; but the most spectacular feat occurred when I let myself be swept away through the rapids and she shouted in fear. They picked me up bleeding a hundred yards farther down. When the trip ended and the raft was packed on top of the jeep, I got dressed among some bushes. Seated on a rock, I was putting on my shoes when she appeared, still in her bathing suit, and told me while looking down: *"Je me veux baigner."* I corrected her: *"Je veux me baigner."* I got up and tried to rape her, but I couldn't.

I made love to her almost by accident. She and I were in a room, alone, speaking of unimportant things, when she asked me; "Such and such an address is in which postal zone?" I didn't know, but I told her to consult the telephone book. She came out of the room after a short time and I heard her calling me. I went to the spot where the telephone was and found her leaning on the book: "Where are the zones?" she asked me. I had forgotten our prior conversation and understood her to be talking about our erogenous zones. I told her where they were located.

We had been born for one another, between the two of us we weighed three hundred fifty pounds. In the months that followed during our passionate and torrid love affair, she called me a buffalo, orangutan and rhinoceros, in essence everything you can call a man without offending him. I was in poverty and she seemed to suffer from constant attacks of diarrhea during her travels through those barbarous regions. At sea level, apart from her need for fourteen hours of sleep each day, she was an acceptable companion, but six thousand feet above sea level she used to breathe with difficulty and fainted easily. Living with her in Mexico City meant remaining in a constant state of alert in order to pick her up from the floor in the event of a fainting spell.

When I discovered her passion for pathology, I invented just to please her a string of sicknesses in my family, which actually has always enjoyed the good health proper to privileged zoological species.

Another of her predilections was something she called "the intricacies of the Mexican mind."

"Do you like motors?" she once asked. "I'm warning you that your answer is going to reveal a national characteristic."

There were certain irregularities in our relationship. For example, she has been the only woman whom I never dared ask to pay for my dinner, in spite of knowing very well that she was swimming in money, which wasn't even hers but came from the Pumpernikel Foundation. With my face in my hands, and elbows on the table at both sides of my coffee cup, I contemplated her for several months as she consumed remarkable amounts of steak and potatoes.

The waiters used to look at me with a certain contempt, believing that I was paying for the steaks. She felt sorry for me at times and treated me to a piece of meat wrapped in a Mexican roll, that I naturally refused, claiming that I wasn't hungry. Furthermore, there was a problem with tips. She supported the theory that one percent was a sufficient amount; therefore, leaving forty centavos for a bill of twenty pesos was extravagant. I had never made so many enemies.

Once I had twenty pesos and I brought her to the Bamerette. We ordered two tequilas.

"The last time I was here," she told me, "I had Scotch, played the guitar, and the waiters thought I was a movie actress."

I never forgave her for that remark.

Her size was another drawback. For example, if you left your arm under her body for two minutes, it would become numb.

The only historical figure that could illustrate our relationship was Siegfried, who crossed the seven circles of fire and reached Brunhilda. Unable to awaken her, he picked her up, found out that she was too heavy and was forced to drag her out like a rolled-up rug.

Oh, Pampa Hash! My adorable, sweet, and ample Pampa!

Her curiosity was terribly scientific.

"Do you love me?"

"Yes."

"Why?"

"I don't know."

"Do you admire me?"

"Yes."

"Why?"

"You are professional, conscientious, and dedicated. I admire those qualities very much."

That last statement was an awful lie. Pampa Hash spent a year in the desert doing research which later resulted in a paper that I could have written in two weeks.

"And just why do you admire those qualities?"

"Let's not be too inquisitive. Let us be carried away by our passions."

"Do you desire me?"

It seemed like an interrogation at a police station.

We went shopping once. I have never seen a more difficult customer than her. She considered everything either too expensive or not good enough, or else it wasn't exactly what she needed. Besides, some mysterious reasoning seemed to convince her that the salesgirls enjoyed ripping the store apart showing their merchandise and later putting it away without having made a single sale.

Panties were almost like the recurring theme of a symphony in our relationship. "I need panties," she told me. I told her how to say it in Spanish. We went to at least ten shops and in every one the same scene was repeated. We would be in front of the salesgirl and she would say, "Necesito . . . " and turn toward me. "How do you say it?" "Pantaletas," I told her. The clerk looked at me for a split second and then went to get the panties. She wanted neither nylon nor silk ones, but rather something made from a material as rare as commercial spider web in Mexico. And she needed them of such an enormous size that it was almost shameful. We never found them. Afterwards, we bought some mangos and ate them seated on park benches. I was fascinated by the way in which she tore off the skin from half the mango with her strong teeth and proceeded to devour the fruit and fibers until the pit resembled Father Hidalgo's head. Later she would firmly pull the remaining half of the mango from the pit and eat it. Right then and there I realized that woman was not for me.

When she had finished her quota of three mangos, she carefully wiped her mouth and hands and lit a cigarette. She settled back in her chair and turning to me smiled and asked, "Do you love me?"

"No," I told her.

Of course she didn't believe me.

The day that rhythm possessed her was the grand finale.

We went to a party where there was a guy who danced so well that people referred to him as the Fred Astaire of the neighborhood. His specialty was dancing alone and contenting himself by watching his feet. After a short time a tropical beat began to play. I was speaking with someone when I got a feeling in the pit of my stomach that something terrible was about to happen. I turned my head and was paralyzed by the sight of Pampa, my Pampa, the woman whom I loved so much, dancing around Fred Astaire as Mata Hari around Shiva. I had never been so ashamed of her since the day she began to sing. "Ay, Cielitou Lindou" in the middle of Juárez Avenue. What could I do? Nothing but lower my head and continue the conversation. The torture lasted for hours.

She later came, knelt down at my feet like a Mary Magdalene and asked me: "Forgive me. I became possessed by that rhythm." I forgave her right there.

We then went to her hotel (with the intention of mutually putting aside our differences) and were already inside the elevator when the manager approached us to find out the number of my room.

I told him I was accompanying the young lady.

"Visits are not permitted after ten," the manager told me.

Pampa Hash became angry.

"What are you insinuating? This man has to come to my room to pick up his suitcase."

"You bring down the suitcase and have him wait for it here."

"I'm not bringing down anything. I'm very tired."

"Then the bellboy will bring it down."

"I won't pay the bellboy anything."

"Young lady, the bellboy is paid by the hotel."

That was the end of the discussion.

The elevator began ascending with the bellboy and Pampa Hash. I was watching her. It was an old-fashioned elevator with iron grills; so when it reached a certain height I could see her panties. I realized then that was the signal. The moment for me to disappear had come.

I was already starting to leave when the manager told me to wait for the suitcase. I waited. Shortly afterwards the bellboy came down and handed me a suitcase that naturally was not mine. I left after having taken it and walked away more hurriedly with each step.

Poor Pampa Hash, she lost me and her suitcase on the same day!

Translated by John Chando

INTIMATE IMAGINATION

The Switchman

JUAN JOSÉ ARREOLA

The stranger arrived, quite out of breath, at the deserted station. His large suitcase, which no one offered to carry, had utterly worn him out. He mopped his face with a handkerchief, shading his eyes with his hands, and stared at the rails that tapered toward the horizon. Winded and preoccupied, he checked his watch: it was just train time.

Someone—where could he have come from?—was tapping him gently. Turning, the stranger found himself face to face with a little old man whom he vaguely identified as a station employee. He carried in one hand a red lantern tiny as a toy. He sized up the traveler with a smile, while the latter questioned him anxiously.

"Excuse me—has the train left yet?"

"You haven't been in these parts long?"

"I've got to get out in a hurry. I'm due in T. first thing in the morning."

"Anyone can see you've missed the whole point of the situation. What you ought to do right off is check in at the Traveler's Hotel." He pointed to an odd, cinder-colored building that would have done as well for a barracks.

"I don't want to rent a room. I want to catch the train out."

"Find yourself a room in a hurry, if there are any still

about. If you get a place, rent it by the month. It'll be cheaper that way, and the service is better."

"Are you out of your mind? I'm due in T. first thing in the morning."

"To tell you the truth, it would serve you right if I just let you figure things out for yourself. But I'll give you a piece of advice."

"Now, look here—"

"This part of the world is famous for its railroads, as you know. Up to now, we haven't been able to work out all the details, but we've done wonders with the printing of timetables and the promotion of tickets. The railroad guidebooks criss-cross every populated area of the country; tickets are being sold to even the most insignificant and out-of-the-way whistle-stops. All we have to do now is to make the trains themselves conform to the indicated schedules—actually get the trains to their stations. That's what people hereabouts are hoping for; meanwhile, we put up with the irregularities of the service, and our patriotism keeps us from any open display of annoyance."

"But is there a train that passes through this city?"

"To say outright that there was would be a plain misstate-ment. As you can see for yourself, we've got the track, though some of it is a little seedy. In some places, the rails are only sketched in lightly on the topsoil with two strokes of a crayon. As a matter of actual fact, no train is really obliged to stop here, but then there is nothing to prevent one from coming if it wants to. In my lifetime, I have seen many trains pass by and known several travelers who have climbed aboard. If you wait for the right moment, maybe I myself will have the honor of helping you aboard a fine coach where you can travel in comfort."

"But will the train get me to T.?"

"And must it be T. and no place else? You ought to congratulate yourself on just getting aboard. Once on the train, your life will take on some sort of workable direction. What does it matter if you don't get to T. in the end?"

"For one thing, my ticket is made out to T. It stands to reason, doesn't it, that I ought to be taken to my destination?"

"There are plenty who would agree with you. In the hotel, you will have a chance to talk with people who have taken every conceivable precaution and bought great batches of tickets. As a general rule, the farsighted ones book passage for every point on the line. Some people have spent whole fortunes on tickets . . ."

"I was under the impression that I needed only one ticket to get me to T. See here—"

"The next fleet of national trains will be built at the expense of a single individual who has just invested a fortune in return-trip tickets for a stretch of rail whose plans, including elaborate tunnels and bridges, haven't even been approved by the corporation engineers."

"But the through train to T.—is it still running?"

"That and a lot more! To tell the truth, there are no end of trains in the country, and passengers are able to use them fairly frequently, considering that there's no regular, out-and-out service to speak of. In other words, no one who boards a train expects to be taken where he really wants to go to."

"How's that?"

"In their eagerness to please the public, the management has been known to take desperate measures in some cases. There are trains running to impassable points. These expeditionary trains take several years to complete their runs sometimes, and the passenger's life undergoes important transformations in the interim. Fatalities are not rare in these instances; so the management, anticipating every possible emergency, has added a funerary car and a burial wagon. Conductors pride themselves on depositing the passenger's cadaver—expensively embalmed—on station platforms stamped on the tickets. Occasionally, these emergency trains make runs over roadbeds lacking a rail. A whole side of a coach will rattle dreadfully as the wheels bump over the crossties. First-class passengers—it is another precaution of the management—are accommodated on the side with the rail. Second-class passengers resign themselves to a bumpy passage. There are stretches with no rails at all—there all passengers suffer equally, till the train rattles itself to pieces in the end."

"Good heavens!"

"I'll tell you something. The little village of F. came into existence through one of these accidents. The train tried to tackle unmanageable terrain. Bogged down by sand, the wheels fouled clear up to the axles. Passengers were thrown together for so long a time that many close friendships grew out of the inevitable chitchat. Some of these friendships soon blossomed into idyls, and the result was F., a progressive village full of cheeky little moppets playing with rusty odds and ends of the train."

"Well! I can't say I care for that sort of thing!"

"You must try to toughen your character—perhaps you will turn out to be a hero. You mustn't assume there are no chances for passengers to demonstrate their bravery or their capacity for sacrifice. Once some two hundred passengers, who shall be nameless, penned one of the most glorious pages in our railroading annals. It so happened that, on a trial run, the engineer discovered a grave omission on the part of our road crew—just in the nick of time. A bridge that should have spanned a gorge was missing from the route. Well, sir, instead of reversing direction, the engineer gave his passengers a little speech and got them to contribute the necessary initiative to go on with the run. Under his spirited direction, the train was disassembled piece by piece and carried on the shoulders of the passengers to the opposite side of the gorge, where the further surprise of a rampaging river awaited them. The result of this feat was so gratifying to the management that it gave up the construction of bridges entirely from then on and allowed an attractive discount to all passengers nervy enough to face up to the additional inconvenience."

"But I'm due in T. first thing in the morning!"

"More power to you! I'm glad to see you stick to your guns. You're a man of conviction, right enough. Get yourself a room at the Traveler's Hotel and take the first train that comes along! At least, do the best you can—there will be thousands to stand in your way. No sooner does a train arrive than the travelers, exasperated by the long delay, burst out of the hotel in a panic and noisily take over the station. Often their incredible recklessness and discourtesy lead to accidents. Instead of boarding the train in an orderly way, they jam together in a pack; to put it mildly, each blocks the other's passage while the train goes off leaving them all in wild disorder on the station platform. The travelers, worn out and frothing at the mouth, curse the general lack of enlightenment and spend much time insulting and belaboring one another."

"And the police don't intervene?"

"Once, the organization of a station militia at all points was attempted, but the unpredictable train schedule made this a useless and exceedingly costly service. Furthermore, the personnel itself showed signs of venality: they protected only the well-to-do passengers, who gave them everything they owned in return for their services, just to get aboard. A special school was established where prospective passengers received lessons in urbanity and a kind of basic training for spending their lives in a train. They were taught the correct procedure for boarding trains even when the vehicle was in motion or cruising at high speed. Still later, they were fitted with a type of armor plate to prevent other passengers from cracking their ribcages."

"But once on the train, are the passenger's troubles over?"

"Relatively, yes. I would only advise you to keep your eyes peeled for the stations. For example, you might easily imagine yourself in T., but find it was only an illusion. To keep things in hand aboard the overpopulated trains, the management finds it necessary to resort to certain expedients. There are stations that are set up for appearance's sake only; they have been posted in the middle of a wilderness and carry the name of important cities. But with a little circumspection it is easy to discover the fraud. They are like stage sets in a theater; the people represented are sawdust facsimiles. These dummies show the wear and tear of the weather, but are sometimes remarkably lifelike: their faces show the signs of infinite exhaustion."

"Thank heavens T. is not too far away!"

"But there are no through trains to T. at the moment. However, it might well be that you could make it to T. first thing in the morning, just as you wish. The railway organization, whatever its shortcomings, doesn't rule out the possibility of a trip without stop-offs. Would you believe it, there are people who haven't even been conscious of any problem in getting to their destination? They buy a ticket to T., a train comes along, they climb aboard, and the next day they hear the conductor announce: 'Train pulling into T.' Without any plotting and planning, they get off and find themselves in T., right enough!"

"Isn't there anything I can do to work it out that way?"

"I should certainly think so! But who's to say if it would really help matters any? Try it, by all means! Get on the train with the fixed purpose of arriving at T. Have nothing to do with the passengers. They will only discourage you with their traveler's tales and look for a chance to publicly denounce you."

"What's that you say?"

"The fact of the matter is that the trains are loaded with spies. These spies—volunteers, for the most part—devote their lives to stirring up the 'constructive spirit' of the management. Sometimes they hardly know what they are saying and talk just for the sake of talking. But the next moment they are ready to impute every possible shade of meaning to a passing phrase, no matter how simple. They know how to ferret out incriminating connotations from the most innocent remarks. One niggling slip of the tongue—and you are likely to be taken into custody; you would then pass the rest of your life in a rolling brig, if you are not actually dumped at a nonexistent station right in the middle of nowhere. Muster all your faith and make your trip; eat as lightly as possible; and don't set foot on the station platform till you see a face you can recognize in T."

"But I don't know a soul in T.!"

"In that case, you must be doubly cautious. There will be many temptations along the way, I can tell you. If you glance out of the train window, you are likely to be trapped by hallucinations. The windows are furnished with ingenious devices that touch off all kinds of delusions in the mind of the passenger. It's easy to be taken in by it all. There is a mechanism of some sort, controlled from the locomotive, that gives the impression, by a combination of noises and movements, that the train is in motion. But the train has actually been at a standstill for weeks on end, while the passengers have been watching alluring landscapes through the windowpanes."

"What's the point of it all?"

"The management has arranged it all with the sensible purpose of reducing the traveler's anxiety and eliminating all sensation of displacement. It is their hope that one day the passengers will leave everything to chance, place themselves in the hands of an omnipotent corporation, and give no thought to where they are going or where they have come from."

"And you—have you traveled the line much?"

"I? I'm only a switchman, sir. To tell the truth, I am a retired switchman, and turn up only once in a while to hark back to the good old days. I never took a trip in my life and never want to. But I hear a lot from the passengers. I know that the trains have given rise to all sorts of communities like the town I mentioned before. Sometimes the train crew will get mysterious orders. They will invite the passengers to disembark, generally under the pretext of admiring the beauties of some particular landmark. They will talk to them about caves, or waterfalls, or famous ruins. 'Fifteen minutes to admire this or that cavern!' the conductor will announce pleasantly. And once the passengers are a comfortable distance away, the train races off full tilt."

"And the passengers?"

"They wander about in confusion from one place to another for a while, but in the end they band together and found colonies. These makeshift halts occur in suitable areas far from civilization and rich in natural resources. Here a choice contingent of young men give themselves up to every conceivable pleasure—chiefly women. How would you like to end up your days in a picturesque hideaway in the company of a pretty young thing?"

The old fellow winked and fixed the traveler with a leer, smiling and benevolent. Just then, a distant whistle was heard.

JUAN JOSÉ ARREOLA

The switchman hopped to attention uneasily and began flashing ridiculous and chaotic signals with his lantern.

"Is this the train?" asked the stranger.

The old-timer began to sprint up the roadbed helter-skelter. When he was a fair way off, he turned about with a cry.

"Good luck to you! You'll make it by tomorrow to that precious station of yours. What did you say your name was?"

"X.," answered the traveler.

The next moment the man had melted into thin air. But the red point of his lantern kept racing and bobbing between the rails, recklessly, toward the oncoming train.

At the other end of the passageway, the locomotive bore down with all the force of a clangorous advent.

Translated by Ben Belitt

The Square

JUAN GARCÍA PONCE

Every afternoon, on leaving his office, C headed for the
square to which he had wanted to go nearly every day of his
childhood with a definite goal in mind, reaching it only on a
few unforgettable occasions. There in the antique ice-cream
parlor under the arcades, to one side of the newspaper and
magazine stands and the ever-changing stills from the films
showing at the old movie house, he would meet a group of
friends sitting in the familiar chairs with metal feet and backs
and worn wooden seats around one of the little round marble-
topped tables. Their number was not always the same, but invariably there was someone. At that hour, the permanent light
that during the day shone down implacably on the laurel trees,
the cupola of the bandstand in the center of the square, the
whitewashed stones of the cathedral and the colonial buildings, with the incongruous rooster hailing the existence of the
pharmacy on one of the corners, began to fade, becoming almost neutral before the sun hid itself from view and for an
instant everything remained immobile and expectant, submerged in itself, as though the moment were going to last
indefinitely and the late afternoon, refusing to surrender to the
night, had extended the day beyond its possibilities. In the ar-
cade the murmur of conversations, the characteristic sound of
a dish on the marble and even the metallic scraping of a chair

on the mosaic sidewalk were muted a little, taking on a deeper note and, all of a sudden, there was heard the excited song of innumerable invisible birds stirring among the shadowed branches of the laurels. Then the slow ringing of the cathedral bells rolled out over the plaza in ever-widening circles and it was as if the sound had induced the air to take on substance by marking itself out in its intangible space like the concentric motion of the waves that an object produces on falling into a calm lake. Meanwhile he ate the guanabana sherbet that the waiter had just left in front of him, idly participating in the vague general conversation. C was dimly aware of that barely perceptible conjunction of movements as something that habit has at last made part of ourselves. Thereupon, time started up again. Before dark, his friends began leaving for home and when night fell other customers occupied the table that they had abandoned with the memory of the ring of one last coin tossed on the marble table top, as chairs were pushed back. Night opened itself to a new day and in the afternoon, on leaving his office, C again headed for the square. And so the weeks and the months went by, one no different from the other in the sameness with which the hours repeated themselves. A wedding, a death, a friend who decided to leave the city, another baptism occasionally gave rise to an unexpected revelation of the passage of time, but, enclosed within a perfectly defined space, it did not seem to be taking on reality by moving forward, provoking, rather, backward looks that inevitably reached a dead end on the appearance of some old memory very soon dispatched to oblivion once more. In the late afternoon, beneath the arcades, the constant changes in the number of friends who gathered together round the little marble-topped table hid the definitive absences, but they were no less real for all that. Only the mysterious change in power of the light, the sudden song of the birds, and the long tolling of the bells remained invariable. That was how one day, carried along by the silent movement of the days which had finally left the table of the old ice-cream parlor almost permanently unoccupied, C too stopped going to the square. The last month, only he and one friend, sometimes two, had continued to meet under the arcades in the late afternoon. Soon the square lay definitely behind. Along with them, the city too left it by the wayside, obeying the involuntary movements that determined its growth. Though nominally it had not lost its symbolic character as a center, and the cathedral, the colonial arches of the palace of government, and the handsome facade of the house on which the escutcheon of the city had been engraved for the first time retained their prestige, to children the sherbets of the old-fashioned ice-cream parlor were no longer the ones most coveted, and among the laurels the bandstand on whose cupola the light settled without reflections as the bells began to ring out exposed to public view its rusty iron railings without its entering anyone's mind to protest, as the stains left by the swallows on the pavement gradually disappeared thanks only to the wind that erased them once the sun had dried them. Isolated in its own reality, the plaza was left without a memory. And to C, who along with the city turned his back on it, his so doing had no outward echo, although beyond his knowledge it had created a vacuum that no one seemed able to fill because it disclosed itself only in the form of sudden attacks of nostalgia for something the nature of which he was unable to express and which he quickly tried to erase, with a sort of shame in the face of the possibility that it would become noticeable and out of fear of the ability of this unknown something to paralyze him in a strange way, alienating him from the concrete realities that were immediately at hand and close to his heart. Nowadays, on leaving his office, he simply headed directly home. There, the mantle of the known enveloped him in its solid folds, though, at times, beneath him, the feeling of emptiness lay crouched, dark and threatening in its mysterious unreality and the trace of the days left behind disclosed itself then in all its profundity though nothing allowed him to recapture them, as meanwhile life or what once hid its emptiness appeared to pass by him without touching him, burning-hot and ice-cold, dense and indifferent, too vague to recognize, too intense to ignore, leaving him alone, helpless, with no one to turn to in order to find himself again, till one day, by chance, C found himself once again in the square in the late afternoon. There alongside him, the cathedral lay in massive repose in the sunlight. The light blurred its silhouette, making it reverberate along with that of the other buildings as though they had all been suddenly set in motion. A few undifferentiated figures were resting on the rickety benches of the square in the shadow of the laurels and as it filtered through the tops of them, that same light vibrating implacably on the buildings formed pools of shadow on the pavement that appeared to communicate with each other when the wind shook the branches of the trees. From the corner where he was about to get into his car, C saw the little marble-topped tables beneath the arcades enclosed within the straight lines of the metal chair backs and headed toward the old ice-cream parlor. As he sat down, his back recognized the trace of the metal chair back being etched upon it, as when he was a child. The waiter greeted him, recognizing him, just as when he had come to the ice-cream parlor on a Sunday morning with his wife and children; but now C saw him in a different way. His face, suddenly grown older, took him back to his immutable childhood desires and his never-recalled habits as a student, halting at a living and unalterable past instead of showing him the path of time. He ordered a sherbet and sat looking toward the square with the sensation of one who is about to enter a room in which everything will prove to be known to him even though he has never been in it. Then, just as when he used to meet with his group of friends and as on all the days that followed during his long absence, the afternoon began to give way before the night and that moment arrived in which for an instant all things hung suspended within themselves; but now C followed each one of the barely perceptible transformations with his spirit arrested at the highest point of an inexpressible elevation that rejected the motion of falling. The birds began to sing, invisible among the branches of the laurels, and then the bells sent forth their dull and prolonged sound above the bird song as though it had not come from the towers of the church but from much farther back, from a different space that washed over C like a vast wave, gentle, silent, and ever greater, extending without limits, as obscure and all-enveloping as a night made of light rather than shadows that had covered him with its quiet mantle. For the first time in a very long time, as he had not felt in the company of anyone or in the face of any event, C felt a silent and permanent happiness, and the square, to which he suddenly knew he would now definitively return every afternoon, was self-contained once again, enclosing everything in a time that is beyond time and for a fleeting but imperishable instant it restored to C all his substance.

Translated by Helen Lane

The Panther

Sergio Pitol

For Elena Poniatowska

No magic permeating my childhood could compare to its apparition. Nothing I'd ever conceived had managed to blend ferocity and refinement so superbly. On the nights that followed I implored, excitedly at first and then impatiently, almost tearfully, for it to show itself again. My mother used to say that if I was going to play bandits all the time, I'd end up dreaming about them. And indeed, by the end of summer vacation my sleep was frequented by the chase and the infamy, the valor and the blood. Back in those days, going to the movies meant taking in a single show, with one film varying only slightly from the next: the ongoing theme was supplied courtesy of the Allied offensive against the Axis hordes. One triple-feature afternoon (spent in wordless delight watching shells rain down over a phantasmagoric Berlin, its structures, vehicles, temples, faces, and palaces blurred under an immense, fiery downpour, epic declarations of love, shadowy bomb shelters in a London of broken obelisks and grand buildings with no facades, and Veronica Lake's tresses, impassibly resisting Nipponese gunfire during the evacuation of a group of wounded soldiers to a big, rocky island in the Pacific) was enough to make the din of bullets invade my room at night, while a multitude of dismembered bodies and nurses' skulls impelled me, in my distress, to seek refuge in my older siblings' bedroom.

Now fully aware of the risks, I invented contrived games that no one found the least bit amusing. I substituted the age-old antagonism between cops and robbers—or the antagonism custom and fashion had more recently consecrated between Germans and Allies—with other beasts, more extravagant protagonists. Games that featured panthers launching surprise attacks on villages, frenzied hunts with panthers howling in pain and fury after being trapped by implacable hunters, bloody battles between panthers and cannibals. But neither these, nor the frequency with which I read jungle adventure stories, could persuade the vision to repeat itself.

Its image persisted during what must actually have been a rather brief period of time. In my indifference, I gradually confirmed that the figure had become more and more feeble and its features, tamely blurred. Time, that headlong rush of recollection and oblivion, destroys our resolve to secure a sensation in our memories forever. There was a pressing need, off and on, to acquire the message my own clumsiness had prevented from being transmitted on the night of its apparition. That enormous, gorgeous animal, whose glossy blackness rivaled that of the night, elegantly traced a path around the room, walked towards me, opened its jaws and then—upon noting the terror this gesture inspired in me—closed them again, offended. It left in the same obscure manner in which it had appeared. For days, I kept kicking myself for my lack of courage. I reproached myself for having ever thought that such a gorgeous beast would ever have any intention of devouring me. Its gaze was kind, beseeching, and its snout seemed more suited for caresses or games than the aftertaste of blood.

New hours took it upon themselves to replace old ones. Different dreams eliminated those that had been my steady passion for so long. Panther games started to seem not only stupid,

but also incomprehensible, since I could no longer clearly recall what had inspired them. I was able to go back to preparing
my lessons, throwing myself into the cultivation of calligraphy
and the passionate administration of lines and colors.

Trivial, joyful, uncouth, intense, diffuse, naively hopeful,
broken, deceptive, somber: twenty years passed before the arrival of last night when, surprisingly enough, as if I were back
in the middle of that savage, childhood dream, I heard once
again an animal panting as it entered the next room. Irrational-
ity, once unleashed within us, can sometimes acquire such a
mad gallop that in our cowardice, we seek shelter under that
moldy set of norms with which we attempt to regulate our
existence, those vacuous canons with which we attempt to halt
the flight of our deepest fancy. Therefore, from inside my
dream, I tried to appeal to a rational explanation: I reasoned
that the noise must have been made by a cat, one that often
visited the kitchen in order to tally up table scraps. I dreamt
that, comforted by this clarification, I fell back to sleep, only
to be reawakened soon after upon perceiving with vivid clarity
its presence quite nearby. There she was, at the foot of the bed,
contemplating me with an expression of delight. I was able to
recall my prior vision within the dream. All those years had
done no more than modify the frame somewhat. The heavy,
dark wood furniture no longer existed, nor did the chandelier
that used to hang over my bed. The walls were now other walls.
Only my expectations and the panther remained the same: as
if merely a few seconds had passed between the two nights.
Jubilation ran through me, mixed in with a bit of fear. I recalled
the incidents of the first visit distinctly, and so attentively, self-
consciously, I remained still, awaiting its message.

The animal was in no hurry. She strolled past me with a
languid stride, then started to make tight circles. Suddenly, she

pounced on the fireplace. There she removed the ash with her front claws, then returned to the center of the room, where she gazed at me, opened up her jaws, and finally decided to speak.

Whatever could be said about the happiness I felt at that moment would only diminish it. My destiny was revealed, crystal clear, through the words of that dark divinity. My sensation of joy reached an intolerable degree of perfection. It was beyond compare. Nothing—not even one of those ephemeral moments, few and far between, in which pleasure foreshadows eternity—has ever produced the same effect achieved by that message.

I awoke in my excitement, and the vision disappeared; however, those prophetic words, written down immediately on a scrap of paper found on the desk, remained as vivid as if they were wrought in iron. After I went back to bed, I couldn't help but understand in dreams that an enigma had been deciphered, a true enigma, and all those obstacles that had reduced my days to boundless time had crumbled to the ground.

The alarm clock sounded. I contemplated with glee the page on which those twelve, enlightening words had been inscribed. Rushing over to read them would have been the easiest course of action, but such immediacy didn't seem proper, given the solemnity of the occasion. Rather than giving in to desire, I headed over to the bathroom. I slowly, carefully dressed myself with forced parsimony. After I'd drunk a cup of coffee, agitated now and trembling slightly, I ran to read the message.

It had taken the panther twenty years to reappear. The amazement she triggered in me on both occasions can't have been gratuitous. The paraphernalia my dream furnished cannot be attributed to mere coincidence. No; it was something in her gaze, above all in her voice, that led me to suppose she was not merely the image of an animal, but the possibility that I could commune with a force and intelligence far beyond that which is human. And yet I must confess, the words I'd written down were no more than an enumeration of dull, trivial nouns that made no sense whatsoever. I feared for my sanity momentarily, then carefully read them again, changing the order of the words as if they were pieces in a puzzle. I joined them all into one very long word; I studied each of its syllables. I invested days and nights in meticulous, sterile, philological combinations. I was able to clarify nothing. Nothing except the certainty that those hidden signs had been corrupted by the same tedium, the same chaos, the same incoherence suffered by everyday events.

However, I trust that one day, the panther will return.

Translated by Tanya Huntington

August Afternoon

In memory of Manuel Michel

You'll never forget that August afternoon. You were fourteen years old, about to finish junior high. You couldn't remember your father, who died not long after you were born. Your mother worked in a travel agency. Every day, from Monday to Friday, she'd wake you up at six-thirty. Left behind were dreams of combat along the seashore, attacks on jungle bastions, disembarkations in enemy territory. And you'd start another day in which you had to live, grow, leave childhood behind. At night, you'd watch television in silence. Then you'd go to your room and read Spanish serial novels from the Bazooka Collection, tales of World War II that idealized battles and allowed you to enter a heroic world where you'd have liked to live.

Your mother's job compelled you to dine at her brother's house. He was surly, undemonstrative, and every month, he demanded your food be paid for promptly. But the presence of your unattainable first cousin, Julia, compensated for all that. Julia studied chemical sciences. She was the only one who gave you your place in the world; not out of love, as you thought at the time, but out of a compassion stirred by the interloper, the orphan with no right to anything at all.

Julia helped you with your homework. She let you listen to her records, music you still can't hear today without remembering her. One night, she took you to the movies. After that, she introduced you to her boyfriend. You've hated Pedro ever since. Julia's university classmate dressed well, and addressed your family on equal footing. You were scared of him, certain that once he was alone with Julia, he would mock you and those little war stories you carried around with you wherever you went. He was irked by the fact that you made your cousin feel sorry for you. He considered you a witness, or an obstacle, most definitely not a rival.

Julia turned twenty on that August afternoon. After lunch, Pedro asked if she wanted a ride in his car past the city limits. You're going with them, your uncle ordered. Sunk down into the back seat, you were dazzled by sunlight and fraught with jealousy. Julia leaned her head on Pedro's shoulder, Pedro drove with one hand so he could put his arm around Julia, a song from back then was vibrating on the radio, the afternoon descended over a city of dust and stone. You watched as the final houses and the military headquarters and the cemeteries vanished through the small window. Then (Julia kissed Pedro: you didn't exist, sunk down into the back seat) the forest, the mountain, pine trees torn apart by light covered your eyes, as if blanketing them to keep out the tears.

Finally, Pedro parked the Ford outside a convent in ruins. He and Julia got out and strolled through galleries filled with moss and echoes. They peered down the stairway of a dark basement. They talked, they whispered, they listened at the walls of a chapel where the stones transmitted voices from one corner to the other. You looked out at the garden, the wet forest, the high mountain vegetation. You no longer felt like the orphan, the interloper, the poor cousin who was doing badly in school and lived in a horrid building in the Escandón neighborhood, but a hero of Dunkirk, Narvik, Tobruk, Midway, Stalingrad, El Alamein, the landing at Normandy, Warsaw,

Monte Cassino, the Ardennes. A captain of the Afrika Korps, a Polish cavalry officer making a heroic, suicidal charge against Hitler's tanks. Rommel, Montgomery, von Rundstedt, Zhukov. You weren't thinking in terms of good guys and bad guys, victims and executioners. To you, all that mattered was valor in the face of danger and victory against the enemy. At that moment, you were the protagonist of the Bazooka Collection, the combatant capable of any warlike action because a damsel would celebrate his feat and his victory would resound forever.

Joy gave way to sorrow. You ran and cleared the hedges and bushes at a single bound while Pedro kissed Julia and held her waist. They went down towards a place where the woods seemed to have been born, next to a stream of icy waters, and a sign that prohibited picking flowers or disturbing animals. Then Julia discovered a squirrel at the top of a pine tree and said: I want to take her home. You can't catch squirrels, Pedro answered, and if anyone tried it, there'd be plenty of forest rangers around to stop him. It occurred to you to say: I'll nab her. And you climbed the tree before Julia could say no.

Your fingers were gouged by the bark, slid on the resin. Then the squirrel climbed even higher. You followed her, placing your feet on a branch. You looked down and saw a forest ranger approaching Pedro who, instead of giving him the slip somehow, started a conversation with him, Julia trying not to look up at you and yet, watching you. Pedro didn't squeal, and the forest ranger, chatting away, didn't raise his eyes. Pedro stretched out the dialogue as far as he could. He wanted to torture you without having to make a single move. Afterwards, he'd portray the whole thing as a prank, and he and Julia would laugh at you. It was a foolproof way of destroying your victory and prolonging your humiliation.

Because ten minutes had already passed. The branch was starting to give. You felt afraid of falling and dying or, worse yet, failing in front of Julia. If you climbed down or asked the forest ranger for help, he'd arrest you and take you away. And the conversation dragged on, and the squirrel at first challenged you from a few inches away, then climbed down and ran off into the forest, while Julia wept, far from Pedro, the forest ranger, the squirrel, but any farther from you, impossible.

Finally the forest ranger took his leave, Pedro pressed a few bills into his hand, and you were able to come down, pale, clumsy, humiliated, with tears Julia should never have seen in your eyes because they proved you were the orphan, the interloper, not the hero of Iwo Jima and Monte Cassino. Pedro's laughter stopped when Julia scolded him quite seriously: How could you. You're such an idiot. I loathe you.

They got back into the automobile. Julia wouldn't let Pedro put his arm around her. No one said a word. Night had already fallen by the time you entered the city. You got out at the first corner that looked familiar. You wandered around for a few hours and, once you got home, told your mother what had happened in the forest. You cried and you burned the entire Bazooka collection, and you never forgot that August afternoon. The last afternoon you ever saw Julia.

Translated by Tanya Huntington

Author Biographies

Octavio Paz (1914-1998) received the Nobel Prize for Literature in 1990, the only Mexican writer so honored to date. Born in Mexico City, Paz began to write at a very early age. In 1943, he moved to the United States, where he became acquainted with American modernist poetry. He entered the Mexican Foreign Service in 1945 and was posted to Paris, where he collaborated on projects with such prominent surrealists as André Breton and Marcel Duchamp. In 1962 Paz was named Mexico's ambassador to India. He resigned from his post in 1968 to protest his government's murderous repression of the student movement in Mexico City.

He later founded two very important literary magazines, *Plural* (1971-1976) and *Vuelta* (1976-1998), and became one of the most brilliant critical and poetic voices of modern Mexico. As an essayist he published many important books, among which *El laberinto de la soledad* [*The Labyrinth of Solitude*] is the most acclaimed and read. In "My Life with the Wave," Paz's short fiction also displays a fine imagination, impeccable prose, and all the other high standards of his poetics.

Carlos Fuentes (1928-) entered the twenty first century as the most celebrated living Mexican writer. An outstanding and innovative author of novels and short stories, he has also established himself as a polemical essayist and indefatigable thinker not just about Mexico, but also on international literature and politics.

Owing to his father's diplomatic career, Fuentes spent his childhood in Chile, Argentina, and Washington, D.C. He published his first novel, *La región más transparente* [*Where the Air Is Clear*], in 1958, and, along with Gabriel García Márquez, Julio Cortázar, Mario Vargas Llosa, and José Donoso, took part in *el boom*, the worldwide 1960s explosion of Latin American literature. His later novels include *Aura* [*Aura*], *La muerte de Artemio Cruz* [*The Death of Artemio Cruz*], and *Gringo viejo* [*The Old Gringo*].

Fuentes is also a prolific short story writer. "Chac-Mool" is but a sampling of his prose, yet it also condenses several universes: the magical pre-Hispanic past and modern reality; everyday, palpable rhythms; and the presence (not always veiled) of the fantastic.

SALVADOR ELIZONDO (1932-2006) was born in Mexico City. He was a man of letters whose superior prose barely harnessed the power and breadth of his imagination. Elizondo was also a tireless reader who provided generous support to more than one author in distress. He was a prolific journalist, a precocious autobiographer, a learned essayist, a lucid translator, an exemplary novelist, and a master of the short story. A lover of cinema, music, and after-dinner conversation, Elizondo was also a bullfighting aficionado.

"History According to Pao Cheng," our chosen story, is just a small taste of Salvador Elizondo's great work, and an example of the universality of the unreal: that unending game of mirrors every writer plays.

FRANCISCO TARIO (1911-1977) was born Francisco Peláez, and could well be considered a strange writer in the best sense. He was a professional soccer player—goalie for the First Division Asturias Club—a passionate moviegoer, and the owner of three cinemas in Acapulco. He stayed on the margins of literary circles despite his friendship with Octavio Paz, José Luis Martínez, and Alí Chumacero, and remained apart from these circles despite being the author of "The Night of Margaret Rose," which is, in the opinion of Gabriel García Márquez, one of the best short stories of the twentieth century.

JUAN DE LA CABADA (1901-1986) was born in Campeche. When he died in Mexico City, he left behind a body of work that, while small, reveals thoroughly Mexican characters and customs. Devoid of moral judgments or ideological considerations, de la Cabada records in blunt prose the course of everyday life, as well as different social classes and their divergences. "The Mist" reminds us that appearances can be deceiving, and that on any given night, we are capable of switching places with ghosts of flesh and blood.

JOSÉ REVUELTAS (1914-1976) was born in Durango and died in Mexico. He was a short story writer, essayist, novelist, playwright, and a champion of social and political causes that led him to endure persecution and imprisonment. An incisive critic, Revueltas deserves greater recognition. As his short story "The Little Doe" demonstrates, he was a prose master who reveals intense emotions and lyrical shades of meaning.

Francisco Rojas González (1903-1951) was an ethnologist and a researcher at the Institute for Social Research at the National Autonomous University of Mexico as well as a contributor to various periodicals, author of two novels, and recipient of the National Prize for Literature in 1944. He is recognized mainly as a short story writer, especially for "The Medicine Man," which depicts both indigenous religions and the unfathomable miracle of chance.

Elena Garro (1916-1998) was born in Puebla and died in Cuernavaca. A woman of extraordinary beauty and first wife of Octavio Paz, she wrote half a dozen novels, among which at least *Los recuerdos del porvenir* [*Recollections of Things to Come*] can be considered a masterpiece. Too little emphasis has been given to the subtle mastery with which she tackled the short story. Her story "Blame the Tlaxcaltecs" interweaves the remote era of the Conquest, a passionate love affair, the memory of an innocent childhood, and the maturity of a fiery imagination.

Alfonso Reyes (1889-1959) cultivated all literary genres. A poet, essayist, literary critic, translator, editor, and short story writer, his vast oeuvre encompasses thirty volumes and made him, in the words of Jorge Luis Borges, "the finest stylist of our century in Spanish prose." Aside from having been a distinguished ambassador of Mexico to both Brazil and Argentina, Reyes was an active promoter of cultural institutions in Mexico, and a generous mentor to quite a few contemporary writers. "The Dinner" is one of the most widely read and celebrated stories by Reyes, perhaps because it confirms the high achievement of his prose while revealing the charm of his wit.

JUAN RULFO (1918-1986) is one of the greatest writers Mexico has ever known, despite the fact that his work was decanted into just two fundamental books: the novel *Pedro Páramo*, published in 1955, and the collection of short stories *El Llano en llamas* [*The Burning Plain*], which includes "Tell Them Not to Kill Me!" This has become a universal story that any human being under the blade of terror can understand. Rulfo won the National Prize for Literature in 1970, and in 1983 he received the Prince of Asturias Prize. But it is the cultural importance, literary transcendence, and heartfelt recognition that new generations of readers continue to bestow upon him that make Rulfo's work immortal.

MARTÍN LUIS GUZMÁN (1887-1976) was born in Chihuahua and died in Mexico City. He was an active participant in the Maderista revolution, joining Pancho Villa's forces. He later went on to become a librarian and editor. Of the two periods he lived in exile, the more productive took place in Spain from 1924 to 1936. Upon his return, he held various public offices, and from 1970 to 1976 he was a senator. In 1958, he received the National Prize for Literature. He is the author of a classic trilogy of the Mexican Revolution: *El águila y la serpiente* [*The Eagle and the Serpent*], *La sombra del caudillo* ["The Shadow of the Leader"], and *Memorias de Pancho Villa* [*Memoirs of Pancho Villa*]. "The Carnival of the Bullets" faithfully distills the essence of the Mexican liberal tradition, as inherited by more than one revolutionary soul.

EDMUNDO VALADÉS (1915-1994) was born in Sonora in 1915, and was one of the few Mexican writers (if not the only one) who actually made his living from short fiction. A contributor to various magazines, he edited *El Cuento*, which he founded and supported, and in its pages published many fine short stories. Valadés was not only a master of the short story, but also the writer who did the most to popularize the form in Mexico. In a single scene, "Permission Granted" summarizes an entire panorama of contemporary Mexican reality. It condenses centuries of history with bittersweet, even irrational wit.

INÉS ARREDONDO (1928-1989) was born in Sinaloa. Her work is now appreciated by many readers who have come to know her in translation. Arredondo received the Xavier Villaurrutia Award in 1979. She will above all be remembered for the high quality of her short stories, faithful to a feminine vision of the intimacies of love. One example of this combination is "The Shunammite," a story that confirms the author's self-description as a writer who took it upon herself to "encounter and try to comprehend souls."

ROSARIO CASTELLANOS (1925-1974) was born in Mexico City, and died tragically in Tel Aviv, where she was serving as Mexico's ambassador to Israel. Her childhood and adolescence were spent in Chiapas, a region reflected in her vast bibliography. She was a poet, novelist, and essayist who also translated Emily Dickinson and Saint-John Perse. Today, Castellanos's works have been translated into many languages. "Cooking Lesson" is consistent with the author's attention to the role of women in the world. It is also a form of protest against the old Mexican *machista,* or sexist tradition, which confined women to resignation, silence, obedience, and the kitchen.

EFRÉN HERNÁNDEZ (1904-1958) and his story "Tachas" share a gift for constant revelation intertwined with mounting amazement. The title of this, his most widely read short story, became the author's nickname, perhaps because his biography and the plot that unfolds in "Tachas" are both so enigmatic. Hernández was born in León, Guanajuato, and died in Mexico City. He is the author of two novels, two books of poetry, one play, and several short stories.

JORGE IBARGÜENGOITIA (1928-1983) may be one of the writers dearest to Mexico, and his tragic death at the Madrid Airport was a great loss to literature. Born in Guanajuato in 1928, Ibargüengoitia amassed a solid body of work in his lifetime, including unforgettable novels, ingenious plays, and entertaining reviews. He was also a master of the short story. Ibargüengoitia wrote clear prose devoid of pedantry or false erudition, and he knew how to use humor and irreverence. In "What Became of Pampa Hash?", Ibargüengoitia's two main characters survive the bewildering and hilarious mishaps of a bizarre love affair.

JUAN JOSÉ ARREOLA (1918-2001) "could have been born anywhere, and in any century," according to Jorge Luis Borges. He was born in Zapotlán el Grande, now Ciudad Guzmán, in the state of Jalisco, and died in Guadalajara. Multifaceted and tireless, Arreola was an endearing man of letters and a voracious reader, a man of unending conversation and constant lucidity. Above all, he dominated the short story. "The Switchman" portrays, in a few short paragraphs, a vast solitude, an age-old illusion, and the proximity of the unreal.

JUAN GARCÍA PONCE (1932-2003) was born in Mérida and died in Mexico City. An exemplary journalist, art critic, playwright, and essayist, García Ponce cultivated aphorisms, novels, essays, poetry and theater in the abundant orchard of his imagination. Though the victim of a rare disease that limited his mobility, in his work García Ponce knew no bounds. "The Square" conveys a kind of public compassion which is not exempt from healthy nostalgia for fleeting, perhaps imperceptible sensations.

SERGIO PITOL (1933-) lives in Xalapa, Veracruz, although he inhabits at least two other worlds: the Europe he toured as an ambassador of Mexico, and the literary world he occupies as both distinguished author and passionate reader. The Cervantes Prize for Literature he received in 2005 is one of various honors acknowledging the superior quality of Pitol's work. Readers revere his books, in which essay, novel, chronicle, and short story are continuously interwoven into a sort of fine cloth. "The Panther" exploits fears that a sensitive soul may harbor, but that few writers would think to set down on paper.

JOSÉ EMILIO PACHECO (1939-) was born in Mexico City. A poet with many important honors to his name, Pacheco is also a generous writer of articles and reviews, a thoughtful essayist, and the author of two brief, gem-like novels. His stature as a poet does not overshadow his mastery of the short story. Rather, Pacheco's poetic language carries over into his stories. As with his other memorable writings, in "August Afternoon," Pacheco evokes the innocence of grownups who disown neither the past nor its magic.

JORGE F. HERNÁNDEZ (1962-) was born in Mexico City. He grew up in Washington, D.C. and lived there until 1976. He completed his graduate studies in history in Madrid, Spain. Mr. Hernández is a novelist and short story writer who has published, among other titles, *La soledad del silencio* ["The Solitude of Silence"] (1996) and *La emperatriz de Lavapiés* ["The Empress of Lavapiés"] (1999). He is currently a tutor of creative writing at the Fundación para las Letras Mexicanas, A.C.

Translated by Tanya Huntington

Permissions Acknowledgements

"The Medicine Man" by Francisco Rojas González, translated by Robert S. Rudder and Gloria Arjona
Of the translation: Copyright © 2000, Latin American Literary Review Press
The translation was published in the book *The Medicine Man*, under the imprint of Latin American Literary Review Press (LALRP), 2000

"Blame the Tlaxcaltecs" by Elena Garro, translated by Ina Cumpiano
Copyright © 2008, Helena Paz Garro, heir to Elena Garro
Of the translation: Copyright © 1990, Arte Público Press-University of Houston
The translation was published in the book *Short Stories by Latin American Women: The Magic and the Real*, edited by Celia Correas de Zapata, under the imprint of Arte Público Press, 1990; it is reprinted here with permission of the publisher

"The Dinner" by Alfonso Reyes, translated by Rick Francis
Copyright © 2008, Alicia Reyes Mota, heir to Alfonso Reyes
Of the translation: Copyright © 1998, Richard Alan Francis
The translation was published in the book *Prospero's Mirror. A Translator's Portfolio of Latin American Short Fiction*, edited by Ilan Stavans, under the imprint of Curbstone Press, 1998

"Tell Them Not to Kill Me!" by Juan Rulfo, translated by George D. Schade
Copyright © 1953, University of Texas Press
Of the translation: Copyright © 1967, renewed 1996, George D. Schade. By permission of the University of Texas Press
The translation was published in the book *The Burning Plain and Other Stories* by Juan Rulfo, under the imprint of University of Texas Press, 1953.

"The Carnival of the Bullets" by Martín Luis Guzmán, translated by Harriet de Onís
Copyright © 2008, heirs of Martín Luis Guzmán
Of the translation: Copyright © 1965, by Doubleday, a division of Random House, Inc.
Copyright © 1930 by Alfred A. Knopf, Inc., a division of Random House, Inc.
Used by permission of Doubleday, a division of Random House, Inc.
The translation was published in the book *The Eagle and the Serpent*.

"Permission Granted" by Edmundo Valadés, translated by Tanya Huntington
Copyright © 2008, Fondo de Cultura Económica
Of the translation: Copyright © 2008, Fondo de Cultura Económica

"The Shunammite" by Inés Arredondo, translated by Alberto Manguel
Copyright © 2008, heirs to Inés Arredondo
Of the translation: Copyright © 1986, Alberto Manguel c/o Guillermo Schavelzon & Asoc. Agencia Literaria, info@schavelzon.com
The translation was published in the book *Other Fires: Short Fiction by Latin American Women*, edited by Alberto Manguel, under the imprint of Clarkson N. Potter Inc., 1986

PERMISSIONS ACKNOWLEDGEMENTS